BOOKS BY RICHARD JESSUP

THE CINCINNATI KID
THE RECREATION HALL
SAILOR
A QUIET VOYAGE HOME

A QUIET VOYAGE HOME

A QUIET VOYAGE HOME

A NOVEL BY
RICHARD JESSUP

Little, Brown and Company — Boston — Toronto

Published simultaneously in Canada
by Little, Brown & Company (Canada) Limited

PRINTED IN THE UNITED STATES OF AMERICA

For John Baldwin
his courage and his laughter . . .

Vera, Marina and Dick

Now let it work. Mischief, thou art afoot,
Take thou what course thou wilt.

Marc   Antony's   address
to the Roman mob . . .

1

"You Wanta Play
Errol Flynn..."

H E WAS A TALL KID, and too thin, and a deceptive gentleness masked the hardness he had acquired at twenty-four. His hair was a jet-black mane that flowed back from his brow and was held there with an old and very worn authentic Apache headband, and because of this he was known as the Indian on the Paris Left Bank, in the cafés and bistros and at the Sorbonne where he was a student. He was not a North American Indian, though he did come from the great Midwest plains.

Indian came out of the bathroom and glanced around the pleasantly cluttered room. "Jeanne?"

"*Oui?*"

"I have to leave now."

"*Merde!*" Her thin reedy voice exploded with exasperation behind the partially closed door of the bathroom. "One moment, *mon cher — !*"

"What are you doing?" Indian demanded.

She said something, but the noise from Rue Gaumont rose to him like a murmur of Arabic prayers he could not understand. The new curtains flew out the window and were then sucked in again and then out again. "Jeanne!" She did not answer and he walked to the phonograph he had bought the year before. "Jeanne!"

"*Mon Indien, chéri, please! Oh merde!*"

Indian dropped the needle into the groove. Piaf spoke her agonies in her harsh, nasal voice; tiresome and sentimental, Indian thought, but alas, true, and universal. He adjusted the volume a little higher and looked out over Paris. The stuttering, gagging cadence of a German tourist bargaining over a one-franc difference in price seemed to fill in perfectly the empty spaces of a deserted Paris in August. He looked out of the window to the stalls below.

The Piaf finished. He sighed in relief. He disliked the woman's singing and suffered it because of Jeanne. He turned from the window and was about to call again when Jeanne appeared. Carrying a box wrapped in silver paper and tied with a clumsy bow of yellow satin ribbon, she came forward flushed with victory. She handed him the box and kissed him. "There!"

"What's this?"

"A present."

"But I am only going overnight." Indian looked at the box. The bow was so very much Jeanne. The ribbon had been pinched in several places, evidence of her attempts to tie the bow more than once. The silver paper was not quite sufficient to cover the entire box and a bit of cardboard peeked out. He looked at her. She stood with a half-smile on her face, bright-eyed, waiting, watching his face, enjoying his chagrin and surprise, silken fine red hair piled messily on top of her head, her lipstick smudged, unaware that her wrap had fallen open.

She threw her arms around him and held him close, breathing a nervous giggle. "I know," she said.

"You know what?"

"That you do not like sentiment. You have told me often enough, *mon cher,* but you must allow a girl —"

"You'll get lipstick on my shirt."

She began to stroke him. She would sit on the couch listening to records and lean her head on his shoulder and stroke him on the arm as though he were a puppy or a kitten. He tried to put her arms down but she held on, and with her fingers laced around the back of his neck she demanded, "Now tell me again."

He tried to look away, to escape, but she held on, smiling, tentative, watching his expression.

"Jeanne —"

"Tell me."

"All right."

She smiled. She snuggled up against him, pressing her face against his chest and waited.

"There were two people," he said.

"You and me."

"And they found each other."

"Yes. You and me. A man and a woman."

"And they found each other," Indian said.

"You said that, *mon cher.*"

"In the rain —"

"Raining *very* hard," Jeanne said. "Oh *mon Indien,* don't you want to tell me?" Her voice was a quiet whisper of sadness.

"Sure. Why not?" He looked around uneasily, guiltily.

"Then tell it the *right* way."

"Jeanne —"

"Tell it the right way," she insisted.

"All right," he said.

She snuggled close to him again. "Now," she said in a child's voice.

"This man, he was a student, was sitting in a café. He was very alone."

"Poor him." Jeanne sighed.

"Yes, poor him." Indian glanced at his watch behind her head.

"Poor, *poor* him." She had begun to cry. She always cried at this point in the story. "He was a student, and alone and did not know anyone —"

"Then he met her," Indian said.

Jeanne wiped away one tear. "Now, tell about her," she said, hugging him again.

"Jeanne —"

She hung on, holding him close. "*Mon Indien* —"

"She was almost as alone as he was," Indian said on top of an exasperated sigh.

"Poor her. Now, tell about her."

"She was almost as alone as he was —"

"You said that — tell it right."

"I'm sorry. Poor him and poor her," Indian said. "They didn't have anyone to love. And when they met each other, they were afraid to love —"

"That's it. But you are going much too fast." She snuggled closer to him. "And they helped each other."

"Yes." He glanced at his watch again.

"Now tell the best part," Jeanne said.

"They are going to have a baby."

"A *bébé!*" Jeanne cried and hugged him with all her strength. "Kiss here —"

He kissed her cheek.

"Here —"

"Jeanne, I must go."

"Kiss here —"

He kissed the other cheek. "There — 'kay?"

7

"Now, *bébé* — umh? One for *bébé*?" She opened her wrap.

He kissed the rounding three-month-old belly.

"Mama and *bébé* thank you, Papa. You can go to your meeting in Le Havre now." She closed her wrap modestly, smiled and turned her back on him.

Indian took the present from the phonograph. At the door they kissed once more and he was out, running down the stairs.

At the street foyer he waited a moment and then knocked on the door of Madame Tumba. He pressed a fistful of francs into the old woman's hand. "The rent —" He nodded toward their rooms above.

"But you are paid, m'sieu." The concierge shook her head. She would never understand Americans.

When he reached the street he looked up and there she was. Jeanne was smiling and waving, holding her wrapper close. She threw him kisses. He waved back and pressed through the crush of tourists around the stalls and hurried into the heat of Paris.

At Boulevard St. Germain he moved toward the Métro with a steady wide stride, his hair flying, and opened Jeanne's present as he walked. He crushed through the tissue paper and withdrew a small papier-mâché daffodil. He looked one time and then threw the box and the paper flower into the gutter. He glanced at his watch. He hoped Scipio would wait for him. He plunged into the Métro.

Indian was one of those children who grew up in the prairie states, Nebraska, Kansas, north through the Dakotas and south through the Texas and Oklahoma panhandles, that have been, for a hundred years or more, virtually isolated from the outside world. They grew up on the ragged edges of a maturing society in which they could barely participate and which they knew little about, except through Hollywood movies, the radio and occasional newspapers. The distances were great, so the desire to travel was not stimulated and was in fact stultified by the dull routine of their lives; as a consequence, their curiosity was usually smothered by the time they were ready to attend college.

Generally, after they grew out of the cowboys-and-Indians stage — or dolls and helping Mama in the kitchen — they gravitated into becoming adults very quickly. It was natural, as right as rain, for them to work and become grown-up while they were still children and receive the blessings and appreciation of their elders for their efforts. It was heady reward to be told you were carrying the load of a man and to begin really to participate in family decisions. Little or no attempt was made to probe the mind and the fantasies of the children. They would continue to live and function on the land as Mama and Papa had done, and by the time they were sixteen they might be allowed to take the truck and drive forty-one miles into Slocum to see a basketball game, read the magazines at the drugstore, flirt for a little bit, and drive home facing church the next morning.

Indian was no different. His isolation from the outside world would produce a very predictable child and his future would be no different from that of any other boy his age. He had books, which he loved, and the movies on Saturday nights, which he loved, and church functions, which he loved more than anything. Like those around him he might go to Iowa State to become an agriculture expert, or Rice to become a teacher, or a good Eastern school like Cornell to become a doctor, or drift almost casually into law at Nebraska, then return to the land and with very little variation function as he had been taught as a child to function — honor the land, neighbors, church, the police and President of the United States — and a great many of his thoughts and ideas and ideals would be those he absorbed from his father, or preacher, or friends, who had learned them in their turn from their fathers.

But one night Indian's father brought home a television set, put an antenna on top of the seventy-five-foot windmill pump, and the whole world that had seemed so far away, so much farther than Slocum and Saturday nights, was brought into the living room. Indian sat in front of the television set for three solid days when it first arrived, and then, groggy-eyed, as if he had eaten a whole pie and would never touch banana cream again, he put it out of his mind; he went back to his books.

When he did return to television once more, it was because of his emerging interest in sports. First baseball, with which he soon grew bored, then basketball, which he disliked because of the constant helter-skelter rushing around of the players, and finally football. Watching professional football on Sunday afternoons became a habit, almost an obsession. There was something in the rough violence of the game that appealed to him. This gradually gave way to his perception that unlike a baseball player, who could — or could not — hit a ball or throw a ball even if he were semiliterate, nearly all the professional football players were college graduates. The more he watched, the clearer the game seemed to him: the violence, the incredible crudeness and brutality that was not really crude, but rather like a game of chess in which all the pieces on the board work together as a team, yet are capable of independent action and decision — while all are controlled by a single mind, in the case of football, the quarterback, or, ultimately, *the coach*. These two in-

dividuals, he saw, had special status. The quarterback was almost never mauled in the junglelike
heaps of arms, legs, bodies, flesh that piled up on the
scrimmage line — and *the coach was never touched.*
Yet it was almost always the quarterback or the
coach who was mobbed for glory and hero worship
when the game was over.

His perceptions drove his curiosity further. He
learned that the coaches rarely came to the game as
former players themselves; that they almost always
made more money; that the nearest they came to
combat was the intellectual tensions they enjoyed, or
suffered, or endured over a *concept* of winning or
losing; and finally, he saw that there were always
eager, faceless, nameless players — *bodies,* with
numbers, almost indistinguishable from each other
— who were willing, eager, *enthusiastic* about doing
what the coach told them to do.

Wanting to learn more about coaches, he went out
for the local high school team with the intention of
getting to know them at first hand. But he wanted
special information — what the coaches *really*
thought about their players. And he learned, the
hard way and painfully. It happened in a spring
practice session. He broke his thumb, and without a
word went to the coach and told him. The coach
called him chicken, challenged him on his pride, his

dignity as a man, his courage, and finally dismissed him as not being worthy to play with his teammates. Indian laughed in his face and walked away.

He knew, for several months after that, that he had come upon something central to his life ahead, but a measurement of its precise value would have to await an opportunity to apply the lesson on his own terms.

Yet there were immediate side-bar values from this experience. The word soon got around that he was not "a team player" and as a result he was shunned by his classmates, and, after making a few unsuccessful attempts to explain his side of it, he withdrew. He knew he was right about the coach, and he was content to let it go. But it annoyed him that no one else understood, and he began to search for explanations. He turned back to television and would sit and listen to news broadcasts and talk shows and documentaries which provided him with a view of the world beyond Slocum High School. And by simply relating what he had learned on the football field to what he heard on television, by the time he was fifteen he had a cynical awareness of the common purposes, the common dynamics, of what he felt to be the deliberately corny behavior and often outright lies a politician told on *Meet the Press* and the lies he heard in church and the lies of the coach. But they were not so much lies, he recognized, as half-truths, shadings of fact, carefully constructed statements and answers through implication. And the politicians, like the coach, *were* the power structure.

The Church, the Grange, the Four-H and students' meetings opened up still another layer of the concept of power structures for him. And from this initial search and discovery he moved on, hardening up, and by the time he was ready to graduate from high school, at sixteen, he was convinced that the power structure of General Motors was no different from that of the Catholic Church or the Mafia or the beloved United States Government.

There was always one man at the top, and a circle of second-raters who were each interchangeable with the man at the top, who supported him, hoping for a shot at the number one spot. In his address as class valedictorian Indian spoke on this subject. There was an audience of seven hundred, with one hundred and two graduating students, but only one person understood that he was making a detailed, penetrating and brilliant analysis of the systems of power structures and their function. That person was Indian. The sad part about this event in Indian's life was that he knew he was the only one who understood what he was talking about.

He had four scholarships offered to him and he

chose the University of Chicago and law because of their accelerated plan for the quick ones. And throughout his college years, there was only one thing that interested him: power structure in all its forms and operations. He read Machiavelli's *The Prince* seven times and found it almost comical that it should remind him of the football coach.

But Indian did not really inject himself emotionally into his subject until he did some graduate work at the University of Paris. At the Sorbonne he met and examined pure anarchy for the first time; not from dry textbooks, or lectures dealing with social statistics, or the moldy diatribes of Marx; it was love. Clean, virginal and stimulating almost beyond endurance. When he met a clever and personable young West German youth at the Sorbonne with ideas which perfectly matched his own, they fell into each other's arms as easily as two boy scouts who have been lost from each other during a summer storm; then his commitment came with the raunchy gut reaction of pulling up paving blocks and hurling them at the police during the Paris insurrection of spring, 1968.

He rarely attended classes. He spent his time at rallies, in the bistros and cafés, and talking, talking, talking; he concentrated on learning how the power structures were oriented. First he wanted to discover

their weaknesses, but he gave that up when he realized that *that* was what the circle of second-raters
were for, to cover up for the top man, to protect *him*,
who in turn protected *them*, and thus kept the structure functioning and intact. He went into a deep
funk when he discovered that each of the second-
raters had *their* circle of supporters, and so on down
the line, creating an invulnerable whole.

But Indian hit pay dirt when he started examining
their fears. There was no way that he could see where
they could successfully protect their fears without
admitting there were fears. And their fear was for
the structure, not themselves. They wrapped themselves in the banners of the establishment and
fought all comers. Popes come and go, the Church
continues. Lenin, Stalin, Khrushchev were only
pauses in the history of the Soviet Union — Soviet
Communism went on. Al Capone, Lucky Luciano,
Vito Genovese were footnotes, mere asterisks in the
Mafia text.

"But isn't that what it's all about?" Jeanne once
asked him. "I mean, for good or evil, *mon cher,* that
is civilization, *n'est-ce pas?*"

Indian brushed the question aside, as he did
everything. He had found it. His quest was resolved
and it fit like a silk glove. Attack . . . attack . . .
attack the established structures.

16

He was ready to put his best theories to the test. All he needed was an issue.

It was a hot morning in Paris, which for many would mean a pleasant day in the country, or at least a stroll in the Bois de Boulogne. The streets and boulevards were filled with people, but they were not Parisians. American, German and Italian tourists, with a few English, crowded the sidewalks. The heat was overwhelming. The noise and chatter of the people in the stalls dealing with the tourists was quarrelsome; there would be no afternoon in the Bois nor picnic in the country for them. The people in the stalls were, Indian knew, the *pieds noirs*, the cast-offs from Algeria. They hoped, by staying in Paris while the Parisian took his August holiday, to establish a foothold. But Indian knew their case was futile.

As far as Avenue de Wagram the temporary stalls were set up to catch the influx of tourists. Women and children hustled the crowds on the sidewalk, screaming the sibilants of their Algerian-influenced Arabic-French, grabbing at the passing men and women in a desperate plea to buy something. The shuffle of sandaled feet and burning leather was a murmur of pain to his ear. He dismissed it all with an annoyed shake of his head. He did not want to

17

think about anything. The Parisian would return and the *pieds noirs* with their strident pleas of self-pity would be driven back to the caves of Montmartre.

Indian lunged on through the shifting crowds. At Wagram and Rue Gounod he found Scipio waiting in the truck. He was pleased to be getting out of Paris. After May and June, there didn't seem to be any reason to stay on.

Scipio greeted him with a wave of his hand. The truck was cranked up. They moved out of Paris. The sky darkened, threatening rain.

"Yeah —" But Indian was not listening. He stared stonily out of the window as the truckdriver sped through the French night with the assurance and abandon of a Saturday night drunk.

"*Comment?*" Scipio's voice was insistent. He turned to look at the thin youth beside him. Strange ones, these Americans. He shrugged. A burly, sweating, laughing man, Scipio made the run from Paris to Le Havre and back twice a week and had done so since the war. He had met Indian a few months before during the May insurrection, when Scipio, as representative of his Communist-controlled striking transport union, had tried to make a pact with the students and Indian had come to negotiate. The negotiations had broken down, but the two men had established a rapport. Scipio had been only too happy to oblige Indian when Indian needed transportation out of Paris. Scipio shrugged again. Indian's silence did not matter. He needed someone to talk to.

"Those were the days, my young friend —"

"What days?" Indian growled.

"Fighting France. We were with the Basque —"

"What about the Nazis?"

"We fought them too, of course."

"But not as hard," Indian said. "You had France in the palm of your hand and you blew it."

"*Comment?*"

"You were shitheads," Indian said.

"*Comment?*"

"Forget it."

They drove on for a half-hour without a word. The surly silence of the youth beside him disturbed the driver. Scipio shrugged it off. *Merde!* What does it matter, a personality? *Phuff!* Scipio blew through his lips. He looked at the boy. But there was something. And when Indian had made the speech to the negotiating committee in Marseilles, even the older ones had listened. It reminded Scipio of himself with the Basque . . .

"There were two brothers. We called them the Brothers Karamazov! They were in charge of one of the red cadres —"

"*Monsieur?*"

"*Oui?*"

"Please." Indian slouched against the window.

Scipio was quiet again, but he could not contain himself. Even if the American was not a Communist, he had a good head. He whistled for a few miles, dodging in and out on the road, warning the private cars in his way with a sharp shrill horn. He cut in hard on several cars and laughed like a child, slapping Indian on the knee with the pleasure of his good fun. He never looked back. Let them get off the road for him.

"Ahh," Scipio breathed, "in the Basque country — I was on the outskirts of Guernica when the Germans bombed it — we were in a terrible position. We could not move —"

"Scared?"

"Scared? What does it mean?"

"Forget it." Indian watched the road.

Scipio continued happily, waving his arms, retelling his great moment. Indian closed his eyes. He had heard the story before. He pressed his head against the glass. The first faint traces of gray had begun to show in the sky. He lit a cigarette and in the glow of the match he saw his reflection.

"So, you are leaving us, eh, *Indien*? Returning to America to start a revolution. Well, they need it. Good luck to you. I tell you, m'sieu, I despise them."

20

"Yeah, I know."

They passed an accident, a head-on collision. Scipio slowed and stared out of the window, but did not stop rolling. A man lay on the ground, and beside him a woman. They both appeared dead. Many cars had stopped. Police lights flashed.

"Groovy," Indian said.

"Comment?"

"C'est tragique."

They rolled on for another hour in silence. Scipio did not try to talk anymore. He was tired and he was tired of the young American. "Le Havre," he grunted and indicated the emerging dawn and the first signs of the city.

"Bon," Indian said. *"Très bon."*

They turned into Avenue Montpellier and rolled through a warehouse district. Silver-sided Renault vans making local deliveries slashed through the mist; hard-rubber-wheeled carts jarred over the cobblestones. At Rue Salle they turned off in the direction of the ship and Indian got a glimpse of the huge vessel laced down with lines in the putrid waters of the Le Havre basin. At Place St. Julien they hit the traffic going to the ship and were promptly stuck in a jam. Rather than wait, Indian opened the door.

"Merci, Scipio."

"Bon voyage, Indien! And if you see Fidel, embrace

21

him for me!" Scipio punctuated his farewell with a laugh.

Indian waved, walked away from the truck, and began working his way to the pier shed. He turned into a side street and the great ship was exposed to him. Black, white, gold, red with blue trim. He pushed through the confusion gathering in the cul-de-sac. There were a great many students and only a few second-class passengers. It was too early for first-class passengers. The S.S. *New York* did not sail until noon.

The students poured through the ship. There was no escaping them or ignoring them. Their noise, their talk, their presence was felt; like driver ants they overran all resistance with their numbers and talk. They argued with the stewards, the waiters, the sailors, their fellow passengers, each other and themselves. The scene shifted, changed, flowed and was groovy — or freaky. Or *stupid*. Or *dumb*. The guitars, the hair, the feet, the dirty, the acid heads, the Che lovers, the Mao lovers, the Ho-Ho-Ho Chi Minh lovers; and all of it thickly overlaid with volume music. Everywhere couples merged, separated, merged again in new combinations.

But this was not Indian's scene, not yet. He moved through the ship with quiet arrogance. He had not bothered to locate his cabin upon boarding the ship.

22

Instead he snagged a cup of coffee in the crew's quarters and then began opening doors and wandering around the ship, examining, questioning, searching, developing a feel for the ship and his new environment. Like a cat sniffing out his new home, he made a survey that was complete and definitive. By the time the ship would be ready to sail, he would be nearly as acquainted with the entire bulk of the great vessel as Captain Coldwater himself. He did not have the feel for the subtleties that Coldwater would have if anything went wrong — or right — in a given area; but he understood function and design, and with what he learned that morning, it was easy for him to construct from the tangible facts a useful and comfortable abstraction.

By the time the one-hour-warning whistle blew, he had most of what he needed. A stunning sensation of excitement surged through his body. He fought it down. He had four days: ninety-six hours. He had much to do.

He plunged into the mainstream of the tourist student section.

The tourist bar was so thick with pot smoke that he began to feel high standing on the edge of the dance floor. The screech of music and human voices joined and mingled into a bedlam like jungle cries —

and with as much meaning. Italian, German,
French, English and American students snapped and
jerked on the dance floor. He watched the activity
coolly. The flower power of Western thought and
culture, he thought. Thank God for the Pill and
American Express. He searched the faces for a familiar one. A dozen people waved to him, greeted
him and smiled, but he did not see a face, a *body*,
that he could use.

Indian moved around the edge of the dance floor,
pushing and being pushed amid the feverish movement. No one seemed to be still. Hundreds of them
were dancing, getting up, sitting down, laughing,
screaming, talking, talking, talking . . . all under
the music's throbbing beat. Indian felt himself getting nervous. He had never really dug the volume
scene. He was tired. He could not remember when he
had slept last. He was about to push his way clear of
the room when a very beautiful and very thin girl
stopped in front of him and touched him, pressing
her hand into his crotch. Her fingers probed.

"You on exhibition, Stud?" she asked. "Are you
passive or active?"

"I've got a hang-up," Indian said. He had not
reacted when she touched him.

"She won't miss you for a half-hour," the girl said.

24

"Here she comes now." Indian moved toward a girl he had seen drifting around alone. "Sorry."

"I have my own cabin," the thin girl said, but Indian was gone.

He pushed through to the lonely girl, put his arm around her waist and pulled her out into the companionway. She looked up at him with remote, vacant eyes. She did not resist. Her arms hung at her sides. She stared.

"You stay right here," Indian said. He touched her heart, her breast. "Stay alive. Keep it beating for me."

"Why?"

"I'll show you later."

The girl blinked twice, slowly. "I don't like to look. I have my fantasies, you know?"

"I'll turn out the light."

"I'm afraid of the dark."

"Stick around. I may have something cooking that will blow your skull."

"I don't like speed."

"What's your name?" Indian asked, squinting in the semidarkness. She was a very pretty girl and her hair was long, down to her waist and the color of the earliest spring forsythia. She wore a pair of blue pajamas and a blue ribbon in her hair. She was small, delicate.

"Some call me this and that," she said. "Cora —"

"We'll see, Cora."

"I'll wait."

"Why don't you like speed?"

"I don't know, drugs are so stupid, you know?" She shrugged.

"We'll see." Indian started to move away.

"I'll wait," Cora said, "if you want me to."

"Wait." And Indian was gone. He moved down through the companionways until he found his cabin. He knocked once, then pushed in. The room was dark, but in the light from the companionway he could see two nude bodies entwined on one of the beds.

"Ralph Rome?" Indian asked.

"Who wants him?"

"Half this pad is mine," Indian said. "G Deck, 703, 'kay?"

"Right," Ralph Rome said, his voice muffled, bringing his head around to face Indian. "Turn on the light and let's have a look at you."

Indian turned on the light. Rome squinted, faced up and stared hard. He paused in his twisting and thrusting. The girl kept her eyes closed. She did not make a sound. Delight and recognition spread over Rome's face. "Hey, the Indian! I didn't know it was going to be me and you —"

26

"Yeah," Indian said. "You know me, huh?"

"Sure! I was in the action around Gare de Lyon last spring, right up there with you on the roof."

"Oh, yeah," Indian said. He did not recognize him. He closed the door and looked around the small cabin, taking possession of it.

"Groovy, Chief!"

"Listen, you about finished?" Indian said in a tone that was both peremptory and authoritative.

"Five minutes," Rome said. He turned his head away. He concentrated. The girl moaned, and responded. Indian stepped out of the cabin and closed the door.

So he was in the Gare de Lyon thing. Indian had needed a body and it looked like he might have one. It was certainly a beginning. Gare de Lyon . . . that was the Bobby Kennedy mixer. They had used his death to take over the trains and they tore out the railyard switches. Good! Maybe, Indian thought, as he worked his way back to Cora, maybe.

Indian and Cora stood on the sundeck and watched the passengers board the great ship. From their vantage point they could look down on the harbor basin. The great gantry cranes on each pier, flying five-ton loads as easily as a spider spinning its web, rose above the sheds and the ships' masts like prehistoric quadrupeds; they hovered over their domain, moving with ease and authority. The sheer physical industrial power of the port thrilled Indian. Now the deep-throated roar of the S.S. *New York* — the half-hour call — boomed out over the harbor basin. The lowest bass note of any ship in the world vibrated against them. There was no avoiding it. They both stood mute and felt its power.

The passengers came. By the dozens and tens of dozens and hundreds. Passengers, well-wishers, families, friends, guests, and more and more students, attended by porters, taxi drivers and private servants; first-class, second-class and tourist. Tour buses disgorged their harried voyagers en masse; taxi drivers yelled at each other and argued with porters; VIP cars were allowed to roll directly onto the pier shed; all, however, were herded politely but determinedly to their respective stations. Pleasure for the vacationer, pain for the departing emigrant, indifference for the student, boredom for the businessman, anger for the air traveler condemned by a bad heart to the luxury of the sea. And everywhere in the confusion the cynical and greedy French porters tyrannized and threatened and manipulated everyone.

Still they came: drunk and hung over, arrogant

and querulous, nervous and cocksure, excited and jaded. This was to be an escape from the world they had known and from which they would now be cut off. There would be no chance of release from the intimate and closed community of the grand vessel for four days. More than thirty-five hundred people milled around in the streets and the pier shed echoing their private worlds of enthusiasm or despair as they faced the voyage; there were as many tears as there were jokes and laughter.

Aboard the ship private farewell parties were under way in the salons, cabins, bars; children raced the passageways and were in turn raced after by unnerved mothers; student couples strode the decks hand in hand; last-minute cablegrams were sent and instructions shouted; pleas for understanding were made and regrets expressed; tearful demands were whispered and tearful promises whispered in reply.

The crew dealt with the confusion with a professionally adjusted purposeful manner that was both gracious and bored. Hidden within the great ship the routine of keeping everything in order continued uninterrupted. The crew moved through its daily chores, watch in and watch out, in an aura of crackling efficiency and assurance. There was nothing new here for them. The passengers were merely to be tolerated from voyage to voyage. The S.S. *New York* belonged to them — to the mates, cadets and engineers; stewards, maids, cooks, sailors, bartenders, waiters, bell pages, bakers, shopkeepers, musicians, lifeguards, entertainers and dustbin porters; boatswains, electricians, carpenters, upholsterers, dishwashers, crew messmen, dry cooks, egg cooks, roast cooks, motion picture projectionist, legal officers, and inventory experts for the dozens of departments; laundrymen and ironers (handwork for the fine blouses and machine work for the bed linen) and masters-at-arms who acted much like Ivy League FBI recruits and who were as polite, deferential and firm; yet all of them and the ship were ruled absolutely by the will of Captain Abraham Coldwater.

And on the passengers came. The last-minute late rushers, those who were chronically late for everything — parties, theater, appointments. Frantic women trying to remember how many pieces of luggage they had while attempting to light a cigarette; men who gave much too much in tips; screaming children afraid to board the ship; and the French porters, hovering like flies, who ployed these late ones as cynically and as surely as a bookie suckers his bettor. Then up the gangway.

"B Deck for Monsieur Dignon —"

"Thanks, pal, but it's Din-yon, and where's the bar?"

She came aboard in a cloud of perfume. "Good morning, Miss Sheaffer; steward, will you take Miss Sheaffer's poodle —"

"Putzi stays with me."

"I'm sorry, Miss Sheaffer. Regulations. All dogs must go to the kennel."

"Where are my bags, I'm leaving the ship —"

"Steward, please put Miss Sheaffer's bags ashore."

But she decided to stay and gave Putzi over to the kennel.

"Good morning, sir —"

Not many more to come now. The sharper, clearer whistles of the tugs alongside broke through the humid forenoon. Longshoremen were poised at bollards fore and aft to throw the lines. The first-class orchestra moved onto the deck and set up their chairs. The leader gave three sharp beats with his hand and a spirited "Hello, Dolly" rang out over the harbor and the pier sheds. Ambitious couples attempted to dance to "Hello, Dolly" and "Mack the Knife," while heavy-hipped women and thin-faced graying men with rimless glasses tapped their toes and watched the fun; *compagnon* singing broke out in the second-class bar; the sweetly sentimental tune made a dissonant contrast with the orchestra's brassy beat. A dozen well-wishers accompanied a departing friend to the gangway and left him standing at the rail while they strolled single file along the pier stringer and sang, turning back to face the voyager, who cried unashamedly as he waved his farewells. A Portuguese fisherman, who claimed he was on a pilgrimage to his father's grave in Provincetown, Massachusetts, was found in one of the lifeboats and handed over to the authorities. The French police promptly cracked him over the head for not answering questions he could not understand. A group of nuns on their way to a Canadian retreat dropped to their knees on the filthy floor of the pier shed and were blessed by a bishop with a whiskey nose and a piercing voice. The porters doffed their hats and crossed themselves, then cheered as the nuns ran up the gangway like excited schoolgirls.

The five-minute whistle blew, obliterating all other sound. The lines were cast off, the tugs took control, the ship began to move, and the S.S. *New York* was under way.

Like a gigantic walled city out of the Middle Ages, with turrets silhouetted against a perfect Normandy sky, pennants flying, thousands of eager warriors lining the railings waving their banners of victory and good-bye, and the whistle blowing *farewell!*, the mighty ship slid away from shore into the wide, dangerous ocean it had always tamed with such ease.

"Come on," Indian said, taking Cora by the hand.

They sat in Cabin 703, G Deck, the door closed, the rock beat from the tourist bar like muffled jungle drums. Ralph Rome and Cora paid no attention to it: they were intent on Indian. He was pacing.

"What we need is an issue," Indian said. "And if we can't find one, we create one."

"For what?" Rome asked.

"Action."

"What *kind* of action?"

"Headline action — the whole world will spread it across their front pages. Violence at Sea!" Indian spread his fingers and made a headline in the air. "Students Riot at Sea!" He paused dramatically. He looked at Rome and Cora.

"You," Rome said, slowly, "are out of your skull."

"You mean you want to —" Cora said, her vacant expression twisting slightly to express emotion.

"Exactly!" Indian said. "We'll take over the ship."

"But that's *mutiny!*" Rome exclaimed. He stood up.

33

The naked girl he had just finished making love to was stretched out in the bed. At his movement, she groaned. They looked at her.

"What's her bag?" Indian asked coldly.

"She dropped acid. Just before we grooved. She likes it that way."

"Who is she?"

"Who the hell knows," Rome said with an annoyed shake of his head. "Let's get back to what you just said. You want to take over the ship. And I say bullshit. It's mutiny."

"No. Student unrest. Lousy food. Cramped conditions. Herded together like cattle. Poor services. Health conditions —" He paused again, his eyes bright, and looked from Cora to Rome and then back to Rome. "Well?"

"And suppose they start shooting?" Rome asked.

"All the better," Indian said. "You remember when the *flics* came on the scene at Gare de Lyon — you remember what happened? There might have been twenty of us on the roof. But as soon as they started shooting, every student in the street, who had been *watching* until that time, was *wasted,* man!"

"Sure, sure, and two kids were hit," Rome said. The nude girl groaned again. Indian looked at her. "She looks pretty young."

"But what's the point?" Cora asked. "I mean, I

don't think it's so lousy, here aboard the ship I mean, you know?"

"The point," Indian said, "is that we have to take advantage of any opportunity we can to make headlines, to make them *listen* to us."

"Why?" Rome asked.

"Because they've done enough, don't you see? They're all shitheads. All of them. Look what the Prince of Camelot did, sending in the Green Berets to Vietnam? And when the Texas Kid had to follow up, do you know what the last count is? Over thirty thousand dead — and two hundred thousand wounded. And who listens to the guy that's getting shot?" Indian paused. "Huh?"

"But the peace talks. They *did* stop the bombing," Cora said.

"You don't *understand!*" Indian said with exasperation. "Listen to me a minute, 'kay? We're going home, right?"

"Right."

"And we have a few alternatives. Either go on to college and get our master's, *or* we enlist, *or* they come and grab us, right?"

"More or less — of course we could go C.O.," Rome said.

"And wind up in Danbury Federal Pen — for what reason?"

35

"But I don't see what one has to do with the other."

"Why did they stop the bombing? Huh?" Indian asked. His eyes were very bright and he had the look of an eagle. He smiled suddenly. Flashing. Brilliant. Complete charm. He slouched, dropped the tone of his voice. "They stopped the bombing because *we* got out and had heads busted and we carried signs —"

"I don't think that had much to, *so* much, to do with it."

"All over the world kids were carrying signs and getting their heads busted — bleed, man, real large *bleed*. I've seen kids *wiped out* —"

"Naw, you don't, Indian. You can't get me into that bag. There are policies —"

"Yes! And who makes the policies? Huh? Why don't they listen to *us*?"

"I don't know; maybe, maybe they've got the muscle, you know? It's votes. You know what I mean? They go for the votes *and* the people who can deliver the votes and get them back into office."

"Exactly!" Indian crowed. "And who has the votes? Not many of us, baby, you can bet your sweet ass on *that*, right? And who winds up doing the fighting, while they sit home and vote and make policy? You know what I mean. Listen, so how many of us can contribute, huh? I ask you, how can we contribute to the shaping of policy, huh? The only recourse we

have is to *create* a *demand* and maybe get a voice in
the continuing succession of presences, which saves
us from becoming shithead lead-bait with their
phony wars and their committed violence against
humanity, and you know who humanity is, don't you,
baby? It's *us*. And they don't care so long as it isn't
them and theirs that's committed. And *how* do we
make our voices felt? Huh? With action, Rome,
baby, with action." Indian's voice had become husky
and emotional. "Headline action. Make them feel
guilty for living. Make them —"

"Think!" Cora said brightly.

"No, you're wrong. They can't think. They're not
intellectuals. Rome has it right when he says they're
after votes to keep them in office. They're just out to
keep their *jobs! My God!* How looney can it *get!* And
here we have a perfect opportunity to *do* something,
and *you* sit here making a dialogue out of everything."

"But this is a ship!" Rome objected. "We're at sea.
And everything I've heard about the sea and ships
and mutiny and that stuff, it's enough to get your ass
shot off; you wanta play Errol Flynn, okay, but for
what reason?"

"You sound like one of them," Indian said coldly.
"You know what I mean, like, man, you're digging

37

that scene!" He watched for signs of guilt, for a backing away from the challenge. It came.

"Ahh, it isn't that, and you know it, Indian. Listen, goddammit, I was *busted* at Gare de Lyon —"

"All right, so you have papers certifying you're not one of them —"

"It's just that —" Rome hesitated. "You know —"

Indian interrupted coldly. "Listen. There's going to be action on this ship. Something to let the world know that we don't believe in their stinking goddamn wars that kill and maim women and children with napalm — or their stinking ghettos — or their goddamn *poverty* programs —"

Cora and Ralph Rome were listening. He talked on. He was remembering coldly the old proverb that the longest part of the journey is made with the first step. They were his first step. And Indian was a superb orator; he used a technique that was not unlike that of a carnival pitchman or a sidewalk barker, starting low key, throwing in a few facts, adjusting his voice to the attention he was receiving, building a phrase or a tone (of contempt or bitterness or indifference), pleading, attacking, withdrawing, yet incessantly soothing and selling, selling, selling . . . "The whole world is about to go up in flames, listen, man, *burn,* you know, and what an-

swers are we getting from our great leaders? Huh,
the same old crap. Promises, and more promises, and
you know what they're doing? They're selling themselves — and at what cost? You know, I mean, at
what cost?" His voice began to press just a little.
"Like that apeshit they had in Chicago, huh? What
about that? And listen to this, just give me a minute
now. Fact. Nixon is going to be the next President of
the country, and I don't have to tell you what *that*
means, now, do I, man? *Nixon*, f'chrissake!" Indian's
voice trembled with contempt. "Fact. If it isn't Nixon,
it's going to be beautiful Humpty Dumpty Hum-
phrey, now that's a superstupid choice, man, you
know?" Indian began to breathe hard and his voice
came out controlled. "And to whom do we have to
look to counter that kind of a choice — Rudd? Huh?
Mark Rudd, f'chrissake! And *Che?* Where the hell is
he? He isn't working for us, that's for damn sure, so
who else, man? One of the great white gurus out of
the fat of middle-age spread — Leary, Mailer — an
acid head and a rich *writer* — are they going to
speak for us? For us, man? I mean, you know — *for
us!* Listen, baby, just listen." Indian's voice became
almost hypnotic. "Let's start something important,
something we can be proud of, here now — let's start
some action —" Indian paused. He backed away. He
rested. "Let's do a war dance home."

39

A QUIET VOYAGE HOME

"All right. Action," Rome said. "Now to the next point. Give me a specific thing we can win."

"We let the guys in Vietnam — *and* in Danbury Federal Pen — know that we're in back of them and their disgust for the things they are forced to do," Indian said.

"So we give 'em a little solace in the foxhole and in solitary. But who's going to say they will even *hear* about it? Jesus, Indian, you want action, I'm your man, but let me have a — let me see, you know, a *point* that we can win. Dig?"

"Suppose," Indian said, still keeping his cool, "our action inspires others? Huh? On other ships? What about that, huh? We disrupt their moneymaking shipping lines and the lines will go to the big policy makers and they'll say, 'Get 'em off the ships, or listen to them,' see how it can work? 'We're losing money!' they'll scream. See it? That's the point we can win."

"Well," Rome said doggedly, "I still don't see what there is to get, here, now."

The nude girl sat upright in bed. She grabbed for her breasts and began to press them. She spoke to someone named Jackie. She flopped back onto the bed.

"She looks pretty young," Indian said.

"I want to know what we can do *now*," Rome said, ignoring the girl.

Indian dropped his cool. He slipped into the charm. He smiled. He stepped forward and patted Rome on the shoulder. "Trust me. It's going to be a hell of a scene. Think of it, man. The greatest ship in the world, and we stop it dead in its tracks. We can get on the radio and broadcast to the world what's going on. We'll have the attention of every government and every radio and every television newscast in the world!"

"And what about the end of the line, huh?" Rome asked. "What about that? When we get to New York and they send in the cops, huh? What then?"

"They can't do a thing to us," Indian said, still charming. "By *then*, we'll have a legitimate issue. And we're students exercising our right of dissent. All we did was *react* to the issue —"

"*What* fucking issue?" Rome demanded, his face congested.

"I'll let you know," Indian said.

2

Jesus,
Sixteen Hundred of Them...

THAT AFTERNOON Indian roamed the ship the way a wounded animal stalks its attacker: sniffing out trails, throwing its nose in the air searching for the scent. When he was rebuffed in his first attempts to get into second and first class, he returned to his cabin, showered, shaved and dressed very carefully, and then made a successful sneak into the French Room in first class. He sat at the end of the bar and nursed a beer and watched and listened and waited. Now he was a hunter waiting for the victim to make a mistake.

That afternoon the French Room was a warm glow of happy talk, laughter and excitement. The room was crowded. Every chair and table and bar stool was occupied. Most of the passengers were still dressed in their boarding clothes, relaxing before dressing for dinner, and now they looked and were looked at; singles very rapidly merging into doubles

45

as the pairing process worked its unerring way. The blonde in yellow went with the skinny fellow in the gray jacket. Indian watched the redhead with the big tits have her pick of three; she chose the older one, the one who looked the richest. The little lady with prematurely gray hair was getting a big play from the French young man with sideburns down to his jawline; the little lady kept stroking the sideburns. It worked. The Italian count was becoming livid at the attentions paid his wife by a very alert and amiable American who had sensed the wife's deep sexuality. Two fags in Cardin jackets, with gold medallions flopping on their chests, made a connection. There were the usual number of highly charged nymphos who were not so careful; and their opposites, the husky males working around the edges like real wolves waiting for the right moment to attack. The gloss, the sheen, the formalized ritual that the game was played with would have done justice to a solemn high-requiem mass. The band, meanwhile, played "Eleanor Rigby" and "Feelin' Groovy" and "Mrs. Robinson" because this was the swinging set and things were moving.

"Another beer, sir?"

"Yeah, another beer, pal," Indian said. Some sort of confusion had just arisen at the entrance of the French Room. Indian watched.

46

"They are students, I believe," the bartender said. "From the tourist section. Trying to crash first class. It happens almost every trip during the late summer."

"Yeah," Indian said. He laughed to himself a little, watching the action at the entrance. His beer arrived. The confusion at the entrance started to get louder now. Several students had forced the doors and broken beyond the stewards. Dressed in dirty slacks, barefoot, stringy-haired, they did not fight so much as they resisted. Indian watched the whole scene critically, analyzing the students' mistakes.

A young girl with a spotty face was grabbed by the arms and dragged out of the room. She grinned and giggled the entire distance to her exit, which took her past two old ladies sipping bourbon, and a dour French gentleman who dropped his hearing aid and started to yell in a hoarse voice using the filthiest of French oaths. The revelers at the bar cheered for the students.

"Leave 'em alone!"

"Yeah, they're just clean-cut American kids!"

"Where'd you get the grass, sweetie?"

"Let 'em have their fun!"

It was not fun for the invading youths. The stewards and waiters and a few deck sailors (called in for the emergency) were quick and thorough. A tall thin

47

young man dressed like a student came in and
started to direct the operations. Indian made a note
of him: plainclothes master-at-arms. He grunted, but
did nothing. He sipped his beer and observed.

Someone upset a tray of drinks. A woman
screamed when one of the resisting youths grabbed
at her fanny and snapped her girdle. A strand of love
beads broke and rolled onto the dance floor like
shattered teeth in a street fight. But finally the invasion was repelled and the students turned away.

Indian sipped his beer. He listened. It was good
fun. The band, damp and pasty-faced in their
maroon jackets, were eager to play request songs,
getting five dollars each number from drunken
suckers. They watched the scene, counted the house,
hoped for big spenders they could con, and played
"Hello, Dolly!" as if they had never heard it before
and might never get a chance to play it again. A faint
delicate haze of resin dust floated above the first
violinist as he zapped away at the strings in his
enthusiasm. The French Room aboard the S.S. *New
York* was living up to its whispered promise in the
Time and *Life* ads: You will be *funned* in the French
Room.

Indian was about to leave when Captain Coldwater came in to inspect the damage and speak to
the headwaiter and the stewards. As a gesture of

goodwill from the Company and the ship, free drinks were offered by the captain. Indian accepted his free beer without comment.

He observed the man. Slablike, thick through the chest — and redolent with authority. Indian liked that. It was one of the fears he had been sniffing out. Take away the power structure behind Captain Coldwater and where was the authority? Yet he was intelligent enough to realize that such a man did not become captain of one of the finest ships in the world because someone in his family owned the company.

He observed Captain Coldwater's handling of the situation with the critical detachment of a field general working out a campaign. Coldwater, from Indian's point of view, had made one mistake. He should have thrown the students into confined quarters right away and then passed the word . . . *cool it!* But Captain Coldwater was thinking about the power structure. The profits. The publicity. The answers to the families of the students. To the members of the board. Mistakes, Captain, Indian thought, watching him, come one to a customer. And a free drink on top of it.

He had found nothing but the obvious. Depressed, his excitement becoming shadowed by genuine fatigue, he went back down below to the tourist section. The invading students were his meat. They had shown themselves to be shitheads. Do anything for a freak, 'kay? Right!

An issue now, just an issue. He had seen enough. In seventy-two hours he, Indian, would destroy the French Room and they wouldn't even know his name.

He heard the screams and the crashing of glasses long before he reached his cabin. But the noise was so loud in all of the tourist section that he did not pay much attention, until he pushed open his door and saw Cora and Ralph Rome trying to control the nude girl. She was obviously having a bad trip. He took in the scene for a moment, hands in his pockets, not caring, wanting to sleep, unconcerned, finding this crisis only an annoyance.

"Help us, f'chrissake!" Rome yelled at him.

"Like what, man?" Indian responded.

"Something. Jesus, she's nuts!"

"Take her to her cabin," Indian said.

"I don't even know her goddamn name!" Rome yelled.

"The doctor!" Cora said, holding the girl by the arm. "Get a doctor —"

The girl threw herself forward and back, lunging, trying to break away from the tight grip Cora and Rome had on her wrists. Her hair down over her face, she threw back her head, snapping her neck hard, and screamed. She was bloody on her stomach where she had fallen into the broken glass. Blood flowed down into her pubic triangle like an arrow. "Jackie — Jackie! *Jackie* —"

"Well, don't just *stand* there!" Cora screamed.

The girl might have been an animal in the stock-yards resisting in its mindless way the death it felt instinctively was so close. Indian did not move. He did not react.

"Jackie — Jackie — take off my skin — quickly, Jackie. I'm full of lice — and disgust. Jackie — *Jackie!*" The girl lunged, she swept Cora to one side and then jerked free of Rome. She stumbled and fell half into Indian's arms, then staggered past him scrambling for the doorknob. But she didn't reach it. The door burst open. The sound of the rock band surged through the open door.

Colonel Algernon Peterson stood framed for a second in the door. He took in the situation. "Eli-enne!" he breathed.

Then he moved. He slammed Indian in the face with an elbow, kicked Rome in the groin and slapped Cora with an open palm, then he had his daughter in his arms.

"Jackie — Jackie — *Jackie!* Disgust — disgust —"

"It's all right, Elly, it's all right, Dad's here, Elly — listen to me." He held his naked daughter in his arms tenderly.

"Jackie — Jackie — please, help me —"

"Jackie is dead, Elly." Colonel Peterson spun around. He looked at Indian who was pushing himself off the bulkhead, wiping blood from his streaming nose.

"What has she taken? What did you give her?" Peterson demanded.

"Cool it, Dad. I don't even know your daughter. *If* she is your daughter."

"What —"

"I mean, like, Dad, she might be your *chick*, you know what I mean?" Indian said. "You might have lured her with a big Honda 750 —"

"My chick!" Colonel Peterson forgot his daughter and lunged at Indian, who did not move.

"You dirty sonofabitch — *slime* — you piece of filth —" Colonel Algernon Peterson had not been trained for nothing. He threw two short chops to the ears, with both fists, like hammers, and then followed with an already swinging, moving elbow and caught Indian on the side of the head. Indian dropped to the deck. Rome responded then. He lunged for Colonel Peterson's back, caught him around the neck, yoked him, and got a stranglehold on the colonel's Adam's apple. Colonel Peterson simply reached back, got a firm hold in Rome's hair and flipped the still naked young man over his shoulder, slamming him against the door.

"Jackie — Jackie —" the girl moaned.

52

Cora whimpered in the corner. Blood pulsed out of her nose from the slap the colonel had given her. She dragged herself to the basin and took a towel to her face. Colonel Peterson snatched a blanket from a bed, wrapped his daughter in it, picked her up in his arms and stepped to the door. He was met there by a crowd of eager, curious faces.

"Get the hell out of the way!" Colonel Algernon Peterson roared. He kicked out. Everyone jumped back.

"Easy, old-timer — you ain't in Vietnam now."

"Will someone help me?" Colonel Peterson said, standing in the companionway, looking at the faces around him. "It's my daughter. Please, someone, help me —"

"Ho-Ho-Ho," someone chanted.

"Ho-Ho-Ho," the voices picked it up. "Ho-Ho-Ho *Chi! Minh!*"

"Help me, goddammit! *I need help!*" Colonel Peterson yelled at them. "Call the ship's doctor, *please!* "We're in A-312 — A Deck 312 — please —"

"Ho-Ho-Ho," the faces around him chanted.

"Let her die in your arms like the kids in Vietnam!" someone shouted. They pressed in close around him. "Napalm — napalm — napalm!"

Colonel Algernon Peterson stepped back. He took a firm grip on his daughter. He kicked out, hard, felt the good solid contact of his foot against flesh. It

53

gave way. He kicked again. Again. He dropped his head and rammed his way through the companionway and ran as fast as he could down the companionway into the foyer where the elevators were. Behind him the chant was a chorus of derision.

"Now you know how it *feels*, man."

"Ho-Ho-Ho-Ho-Ho-HO-HO-HO-HO-HO!"

They followed him to the foyer. It took several of the masters-at-arms and six waiters to get Colonel Peterson and his daughter into the elevator. Indian watched coolly, wiping his bloody nose, until the elevator doors closed behind them.

"Jackie — the lice, Jackie — Jackie — the *lice!*" the girl screamed.

"It's all right, Elly, it's all right," Colonel Peterson repeated.

Once they had gotten everyone out of the cabin and they had stopped the flow of blood, Indian sat quietly on the side of the bed with a towel pressed against his nose. He did not show it, but something had exploded inside his brain like a signal flare.

He had his issue.

His tiredness, his tensions, his gut drive fell away from him and he relaxed. "Right," he said briskly, examining the towel. He stood. He observed Rome's efforts with the still bleeding and near-hysterical

Cora and he took command of the situation with the serenity of a reassuring mother.

"Easy with her now. That's a pretty bad bust in the nose, Cora. Your first badge of honor in the revolution — hold her, Rome, that's it. Easy, okay, baby, you've earned letters, spades and a Jesus pin from Sunday school."

Indian felt the girl's nose. He did not think it was broken. "Can you breathe freely?"

"Yes — except for the blood — it keeps going into my throat."

"It'll stop soon," Indian soothed. He sat on the side of the bed, holding Cora's hand. " 'Kay?"

She nodded. She tried to smile, and gagged.

"What do we do now?" Rome wanted to know. He massaged his shoulder where he had landed on the deck and twisted against the door.

"It won't be long."

"For what?" Rome demanded.

"The master-at-arms will be down. That was a full colonel. A chicken colonel with a Green Beret: tough, as you well know —"

"What the fuck is going to happen now?"

"Where did you meet the girl?"

"Wandering around in the bar," Rome said.

"She looked pretty young."

"So what? She had already dropped the acid. I just

took advantage of something any other stud would have done."

Indian looked at Cora. She seemed to be quiet. He quickly ran through the possibilities, the probabilities and the alternatives.

"Right," he said coolly. "Let me take the bust. You and Cora — do you have a cabin, Cora?"

"G-514."

"You and Cora — go, *now*, to her cabin. Get the hell out of here. Stay out of sight. Go underground, until you hear from me. Don't talk to anyone. Absolutely no one, especially the Ho-Ho-Ho groups, get me?"

Rome was so relieved to be shielded from another meeting with the colonel that he didn't even ask any questions.

"Move it!" Indian said. "Clean out everything you own."

Rome did not hesitate. He grabbed his clothes and dressed hurriedly. He collected Cora and his one suitcase, opened the door and slipped out of the cabin.

Indian stood. He worked quickly to clean up the mess the fight had created. He was sweeping broken glass when there was a tap on the door; it opened before he could speak.

"Yes?"

Three men stood outside. They were a little older than Indian, heavier, with square solid faces. They wore web belts and pistols. They came inside and, without any words at all, took Indian into custody. He did not resist and went with them willingly.

"Please take me to the hospital," Indian said. "I need medical assistance. And I wish to lodge a protest against the colonel for assault."

Indian sneezed deliberately. Blood flowed out of his nose and onto the pristine white uniforms of the three masters-at-arms.

"Dr. Jaca?"

"Yes, who is this?"

"Alexs. Listen, I can't find the captain anyplace. And I've just gotten a call from below. A Colonel Peterson, First Class, Army, Green Beret, is traveling with his daughter and one of those goony kids made the mistake of screwing her; the colonel roughed the kid up pretty badly; and the girl is out —"

"Just a minute, Alexs," Dr. Jaca said. "I think one of them is here now."

"Which one?"

"A young man."

"Listen, Doc, never mind the kid, take care of the girl. There is something else —"

57

Dr. Jaca watched Indian holding the bloody towel to his nose. "Make it snappy, Alexs."

"Those goddamn kids!" the voice exploded in Dr. Jaca's ear. "Sixteen hundred of them —"

"Alexs — save it!" Dr. Jaca said sharply. "Tell me about the problems of the purser some other time. What was there about the girl, beyond the cut?"

"We're pretty sure it's LSD."

"Oh Christ." Dr. Jaca dropped the phone in the cradle and turned to Indian. "Sit down over there and hold your head back."

"I'd like to speak to the captain please," Indian said, sitting down. "I was assaulted —"

"Don't talk," Dr. Jaca said. He examined Indian's nose. He felt for disrupted cartilage, found none, then noticed a slight swelling and redness around both ears. "What happened here?" he asked and touched one ear carefully. Indian winced.

"The colonel — he hammered me — judo, I guess." Indian made two fists and brought them together.

Dr. Jaca grunted. Internal pressure. He moved rapidly to restrict the hemorrhage. "Don't talk and don't move," Dr. Jaca said sternly to Indian. He turned to the three masters-at-arms who stood around stiffly in the crowded hospital. "Outside, please."

"He's in custody, Dr. Jaca."

"Right now he's in my custody. Stand outside." He looked around. It was typical of the first few hours after sailing; and this trip, only slightly bad weather had produced a scene that reminded him of a field aid station. The hospital and dispensary were nearly full. And the sweet-sour smell of vomit was thickening. Two deck sailors wearing face masks mopped the floor. The sea drunks, Jaca knew, were only passing illnesses: too much champagne and too much liquor, once there was a slight pitch or roll to the ship's motion, positively ravaged the stomach. He cursed under his breath.

"Jackie — *Jackie* —" A screaming wail filled the room.

Jaca snapped around. Colonel Peterson stood beside a stretcher carried by two sailors. "Outside!" he ordered, looking at the colonel.

"She's my daughter," Colonel Peterson said.

"Take her into the emergency room," Jaca directed the sailors. "Carol!"

The nurse responded immediately. "Doctor?"

"They've drugged her — and raped her — they —" Colonel Peterson held Jaca by the arm.

"Take this man out of here," Jaca said to the masters-at-arms.

"Please, sir." One of them stepped inside and took

Colonel Peterson by the arm. Peterson turned away, accepting the logic, and then saw Indian.

"You bastard." Colonel Peterson took one step forward; he slapped Indian with his open palm, knocking him off the chair and upsetting a small table. Someone screamed.

"Restrain that man!" Jaca shouted above the noise. Other patients who had gathered to watch shrank back. A young girl began to vomit. Indian was on the floor, out cold, his head against the bulkhead. The masters-at-arms hustled Colonel Peterson out of the room and down the companionway.

Indian was picked up by two of the swabbing deck sailors and placed on a chair. The nurse crushed a vial of ammonia; Indian began to come around. Jaca checked his nose briefly. The bleeding had stopped.

"Hold him up," Jaca ordered one of the sailors. "Keep him quiet."

"Yes, sir."

"Carol!" Jaca hurried into the emergency room.

The girl writhed and twisted and pulled at her skin. "Jackie — Jackie — *Jackie — the lice!*"

"Restraints!" Jaca ordered. He prepared a syringe while Carol strapped Elienne Peterson down to the table. He stepped to the girl's side and made an injection, a simple sedative that would counteract the LSD. He threw the syringe to the floor in a moment of outrage and disgust at what humanity did to itself. He moved in over the table and examined the wound.

"Carol —"

Jaca worked quickly. Clamp. Open the wound. Lay back the layers of tissue. Clamp. Muscle, fat, there! How lucky you are, young lady, Jaca thought, glancing at the pale face. Another eighth of an inch and you could have been in serious trouble for the rest of your life. He concentrated his mind wholly on closing the wound. Healthy young muscle — suture — remove the clamps. Finished! You're going to have a nice flashy scar, my pretty. I wonder what you will tell your husband.

"That was marvelous, Dr. Jaca," the nurse said.

"All right, let's check her out."

He went through the ritual quickly, easily. He stepped back. "My God —"

"What is it?" Carol moved to his side.

Elienne Peterson lay on the table, pale, calming, her eyes wide open. She spoke, a whisper, nearly asleep. "Jackie — Jackie?"

"She's pregnant," Jaca said. "At least three months."

Indian sat outside Captain Coldwater's suite just below the bridge deck. His head pounded, but the doctor had given him a mild sedative and the pain was now just beginning to ease off. The captain's secretary sat behind a desk and shuffled papers and answered telephones and now and then glanced at Indian. A steady flow of visitors and ship's crew conducting business moved in and out on deep carpets. Stern, the captain's steward, came out once and asked Indian if he was comfortable and would he like a cup of coffee or tea. Indian accepted tea.

The purser, Alexs, came and checked something with the secretary, glanced at Indian and left. Then Dr. Jaca came, looking tired and overworked, and sat down opposite Indian.

"How do you feel?" Dr. Jaca asked.

"Okay, I guess. Are you waiting for the captain?"

"Yes."

"Something to do with me — this situation?" Indian asked.

"Yes."

"You have a slight Spanish accent," Indian said.

"You have a good ear," Jaca said. "Are you a linguist?"

"No, not really. In my work, my studies, I've had to learn a smattering."

"What is your work?" Jaca asked.

"Student," Indian said simply.

"Of what?"

"Are you Spanish?" Indian asked.

"Cuban."

"You're not more than forty, let's see, ten years," Indian said speculatively. "That would make you a doctor under Batista."

"Do you always do this?"

"What?"

"Answer a question with a speculative question."

Indian's eyes narrowed. He shifted his position. "You have had experience with dialectical discussions, haven't you?"

"Hasn't every, ah, student?" Jaca asked, smiling.

Indian flushed. "You're very good," he said.

"As a doctor, yes. I have my vanity," Jaca said; he nodded, interested. "But —"

"You know what I mean," Indian said harshly.

"Don't be foolish," Jaca said. "You're a very young man — and in serious trouble."

"Why did you leave Cuba? Did you know Fidel — Che?"

"And you're arrogant," Jaca said. "Quite arrogant. And, yes, I knew them both."

"You ran."

"Not at all."

"I also hear Harvard — Cuban, Harvard. Now working on a ship. What happened to you, Doctor? Something bust you?"

"Harvard?"

63

"I *hear* Harvard, Doctor," Indian said.

"Then you'd better hear this. Colonel Peterson is not a man to be trifled with."

"He assaulted me!" Indian said firmly. "You saw him."

"And before that? What did you do to his daughter?"

"I never saw her before in my life. I opened the door to my cabin and there she was, freaked out — dig?"

"You didn't sleep with her?"

"Come'n, Doc. With all the chicks wandering around loose down below, why would I go for an acid head?"

"Another question answered with a question," Jaca said. "You are very tiresome."

"Cuban," Indian said. "Cuban fascist — or Cuban coward?"

Jaca looked at him steadily a moment. He shook his head. He puffed on a cigarette.

"No answer, Doctor? Nothing to say?"

Jaca looked at him.

"Perhaps you were revolutionary in sympathies, how's that? But didn't want to have the restrictions; you know, too used to your upper-middle-class creature comforts? So you split. Huh?"

Jaca felt the blood rush to his face. "We," he said

very slowly, deliberately implying that the "we" included Fidel and Che, "used to chew the young ones like you with our front teeth and spit them out."

"Ahh! So you did participate. I've always enjoyed talking to second-raters, people like yourself, you know, man, revolutionaries who failed, or didn't have the feel for the action." Indian smiled. "Dig?"

"Dig," Jaca said. "Come back and talk to me in five years."

"Five years is all the way out, man, like a dissolve, you know? Who would be interested in you, after five years?"

"No one," Jaca said. "No one at all."

"Right."

"Dig?" Jaca asked, suddenly, sharply, catching Indian off guard.

"Dig?"

"You're a talker," Jaca said. "A modern-style revolutionary who talks and does not fight. A spin-off of the Real Thing, who doesn't have anything but a big mouth —"

"Don't get *emotional,* man," Indian said coolly. "You're getting, I mean, *up tight!*"

"Talker," Jaca said. "You let a simple little thing like an outraged father almost scramble your brains. You'd better be careful, talker, you might get in the way of something stronger."

65

"Like what?" Indian said. He was cool, very cool. He was pretty sure he had found a patsy. "Like what, man?"

Jaca slumped. He was genuinely tired. Why had he let a boorish young man reach him? He shrugged. He looked at Indian and smiled.

Indian wiped his nose. Old revolutionaries were the easiest of all to take. They came charging out like punch-drunk fighters. All you had to do was ring the bell and there they were. And so easy to lay off on. He looked at Jaca. Patsy. A-1 first class. Groovy.

"You may go in now, Dr. Jaca," the secretary said. "And you as well." He looked at Indian.

Captain Abraham Coldwater arose from behind his desk as they came in. He was angry, with the sullen temper of a man who is tired but for some minor reason cannot quit work to rest. What he wanted — what he needed — was an icy shower and a drink, and he wanted them right now. But there sat Colonel Peterson — and the colonel was justly outraged, Coldwater knew, but he had listened to too much of what the colonel had had to say.

"How is my daughter, Doctor?" Colonel Peterson was on his feet. Then he saw Indian. He reddened. "Do we have to have him here?" He looked at Captain Coldwater.

66

"Your daughter is sleeping," Jaca said. "I won't know anything until later — tomorrow perhaps when the effects of the LSD wear off."

"Just a minute!" Indian said sharply. "There seems to be something missing here."

Coldwater and Peterson frowned. Jaca turned slowly and stared at Indian. He stared a long time, thoughtfully, then shrugged.

"What is it you think is missing?" Coldwater asked.

"My side," Indian said.

"Your side?" Coldwater repeated. "What do you think this is? A trial?"

"I don't know, but you've had private conversation with this man," Indian indicated Colonel Peterson, "who assaulted me —"

"And what did you do to my daughter?" Peterson demanded.

"Nothing, baby, nothing at all. I never saw your daughter one single minute before I stepped in my cabin and found two freaky kids trying to *control* your daughter — then *you* came in, uninvited, and beat hell out of everyone in sight."

"Who were the others?" Coldwater asked.

"Never saw them before in my life."

"Wasn't one of them your roommate — sharing your cabin?" Coldwater asked.

"I haven't *seen* my roommate, man."

"Captain, if you please," Coldwater said quietly but firmly.

"You're a goddamned liar!" Peterson said heatedly.

"You're getting flakey, soldier," Indian said. "And if you touch me again, you sonofabitch, I'll beat you to death with a chair." Indian's voice was quiet. "You've assaulted *me twice*, remember that."

"What!" Peterson stopped and stared.

"Now none of that," Coldwater said coldly.

"Well, when do I get a chance to lay it on the Green Beret here, *Captain*? Or is it that I'm a student so I can be manhandled? Huh, which is it, *Captain*?"

Jaca sat to one side, smoking, watching Indian intently. It all seemed weirdly familiar to him. The outrage, the emotion, the aimless, often interrupted talk on one side being coldly fragmented by a single destructive mind on the other. He had heard it before.

"You have rights," Coldwater said tiredly. "I guarantee them."

"Then what is this all about? Why am I here?" Indian demanded.

"You're here because I accuse you of giving my daughter drugs and then, when she was under the influence, you raped her!" Colonel Peterson half stood.

68

"Am I being charged with this, Captain?"

"Not at all. I want to get to the bottom of this," Coldwater said. "And, Colonel Peterson, I would appreciate it if you would remain silent."

"Who is going to determine what is the bottom, Captain?" Indian asked quietly.

"Me."

"To what end, sir?"

"If you have committed a crime, you will be confined and handed over to the authorities when we reach New York —"

"And *his* crime?" Indian jabbed a finger in the air toward Colonel Peterson.

"*My* crime?" Peterson shouted.

"Actually, Captain, I was attempting to help Colonel Peterson's daughter —"

"By raping her!" Colonel Peterson shouted again.

"I never touched your daughter."

"You were attempting to assist Miss Peterson, is that your story?" Coldwater asked.

"It's not *story*, Captain. It's fact."

"Can you prove what you say?" Coldwater asked.

"Can he prove his story and accusations?" Indian looked at Peterson. "I doubt it. I seriously do. I think he's got a goony daughter who freaked out while he was off to the wars bombing innocent children with napalm —"

69

There was a moment of silence. Peterson and Coldwater stared at Indian, neither of them moving. Only Jaca moved: He lit another cigarette and exhaled. Some instinct warned him that Indian had something. He was too cool. Jaca waited.

Colonel Algernon Peterson had a stunned look. He visibly sagged. He turned and looked at Coldwater. "Where do they come from? What's happening to the world? I hold the Congressional Medal of Honor — I am a distinguished and honorable man — I — I don't understand."

"I think you owe Colonel Peterson an apology," Coldwater said.

"For what?" Indian demanded harshly.

"No, no — I don't want his apology. But I would like to know why?"

"Why what?" Indian demanded in the same harsh voice.

"Why you would want to corrupt an innocent little girl — why? Why destroy her?"

"*What* innocent little girl?" Indian asked, again.

Jaca straightened up. He felt his nerves tingle. Yes, this was the kill. He's going to gut them now. He hunched forward and watched Indian, who had not moved, but stood in the same spot since he had entered.

"*My* innocent little girl!" Peterson said like a man

strangling in his own blood. "My daughter! Why did you — all of you —"

"Your daughter is not innocent," Indian said flatly.

"What — what do you mean?" Peterson demanded.

Jaca hunched forward. He realized he was actually excited.

"Your daughter is pregnant," Indian said. "Three months."

Colonel Peterson lunged for Indian and grabbed him by the throat. Indian twisted away; then Jaca and Coldwater had Peterson by the arms and pulled him back.

Peterson relaxed. He stared at Indian, pure disbelief in his gray eyes. "You rotten — you disgusting evil thing."

"Ask the doctor," Indian said.

Jaca felt himself let go inside. Of course, the trap move. Suck them in and gut them with their own virtues. Of course the kid had overheard Carol and himself discuss it. Carol would not have told him.

"It's true," Jaca said unwillingly. "Your daughter is pregnant. I'm sorry —"

"I don't believe it —" Peterson looked at Jaca, his mouth open. He nearly gasped for breath. "But how could she — I mean —"

Coldwater motioned Jaca to take Indian out of the

room. As they walked out he rang for the steward. "Bring the colonel a drink, Stern. Bourbon." He went to the colonel's side and put his hand on his shoulder. "I'm sorry, Colonel. I am."

Colonel Peterson did not respond. He stared in front of him. Very slowly he began to shake.

Coldwater waved Stern away and both of them left the colonel alone. They closed the door on a sob. It was the most horrifying sound Captain Coldwater had ever heard in his life. Then he looked at Indian and thought about Vietnam. And napalm.

Indian and Jaca stood at one side of the anteroom. Coldwater walked over to them. He looked at Indian a long time. "All right, it's all over. Go below. And if there's anymore trouble, I'll take care of it myself, personally."

"It's not over," Indian said with a level gaze.

Jaca moved away a little and observed Indian again, picking up every vibration.

"It's over," Coldwater said firmly. "Get below."

"Has all of this been recorded in the ship's log?" Indian demanded.

"It has," Coldwater replied, a deepening dangerous tone creeping into his voice.

"Thank you, Captain," Indian said, suddenly smiling and turning away.

"Jesus!" Coldwater breathed. "Sixteen hundred of

them. And that poor man inside — well! Thank God
I don't have to understand them. Stern! Stern! *Goddammit!*"

"Right here, sir."

"I want a split of Dom Perignon, and I want it cold
enough to freeze a private's ass at Valley Forge —
I'll take it on the lee bridge. Let the colonel alone,
he'll leave when he's ready. Jesus! Three months'
pregnant, huh, Jaca? Are you sure?"

"Three months."

"How old is she?"

"Not more than sixteen would be my guess."

"That young man is very lucky," Coldwater said.

As all revolutionaries are lucky, when they win,
Jaca thought. But how many win? Jaca shrugged,
remembering the last time he had seen Che — the
loser. Fidel, the winner, had sent Che to get Jaca to
join them in the hills. At first there had been a lot of
polite talk, until Jaca refused to go with him; then it
had gotten nasty. Che had become imperious, point-
ing his finger, but keeping his voice down low and
cool. There was a lot of Che in Indian. He sighed. A
lot of Fidel, too. He sighed again. To hell with them
all. He picked up the phone and asked for the hospital, glad that he was out of it all, that for him it was
over.

"How are things?"

"Quiet. Few more sea drunks. And a Miss Gloria Sheaffer called, inviting you to a cocktail party."

"Call back and tell her I'll come if I don't have to get into dress whites. Explain about sailing day —"

"Will do."

"How's the Peterson girl?"

"Out. Cold."

"Good. Watch her. And tell Kenneth to watch for restlessness when he relieves you."

"Will do."

"And keep Colonel Peterson away from her. No visitors until I have had a chance to talk to her — that is if she wakes up. The wrong question or approach after a psycho-trauma like she's had and it could jar her right into oblivion . . ."

"Yes, Doctor."

Jaca needed air. He hurried to the boat deck and found an isolated spot. The sea calmed him. The English Channel afternoon was fading, and, though he could not see it, he knew that the Cornwall coasts and the beaches of Penzance were tinged with a pale cast of orange. Dorset, he thought. Dorset would be lovely now.

But Havana would be beautiful, exquisite with color. Havana . . .

"Good evening, Dr. Jaca."

Jaca turned. "Oh, hello, Trapp. How's it going?"

74

"So-so."

"You sound down," Jaca said, turning back to the railing and the water. He liked the young officer. Trapp's stated and sole purpose for going to sea was to meet and marry a rich and beautiful woman. "Any possibilities this trip?"

"A few possibles and a pretty good maybe. The maybe is Texas. Oil, traveling with her current husband."

"Good luck." Jaca chuckled.

"Say, that kid, the one the colonel busted up?"

"Yeah?"

"He's down in tourist making a — I guess you'd call it a radical speech."

"Oh? I'm not surprised," Jaca said.

"Yeah. Spouting off about life being meaningless and that the greatest life that was ever lived was —" Trapp paused.

"Wasted," Jaca said and flipped his cigarette over the side. "Wasted, for not seeing the alternatives. So! The argument is against society and its ignorance of the alternatives, and a condemnation of the power structures for not taking the lower social orders to their hearts. The present criteria are not the only ones. If we would just look around us and *act* on what we see —"

75

"Say, that's it!" Trapp said, impressed. "You heard it too, huh?"

"No, just happened to have read the same book. Nonti Osorio, *Fourth Dialogues* — see you, Trapp. Good luck with Texas."

"Sure," Trapp said. "Sure, Doc."

Che — Fidel — Nonti Osorio — and the one they called Indian, he could not remember his name — Maynard Something — all of it coming together at one time. The old emotion was there, still; not as fevered perhaps, but alive. He would never have thought so.

At six-thirty everything was going smoothly for Indian. He stood alone on the deck, facing the cold wind, letting it blow his head clear. The ship's whistle boomed out over the darkening waters. There was a small craft, fat, round, sailing shoreward into a failing breeze. A skinny youth in white ducks and long hair was intent on his sailing while a girl huddled in the bow. She looked cold, Indian thought.

Indian was biding time: he could not move into the first phase until the ship was well out to sea, far beyond the possibility of the captain doing something foolish like calling in the English Coast Guard — or even turning back.

He looked out at the darkening sky and sea. The ship had a gentle roll to it and it comforted him. He felt calm and peaceful. It would be simple enough to provoke Colonel Peterson into another attack on him — or anyone — and then he would be ready to move. Coldwater had trapped himself by treating Peterson as a fellow member of the club, the group, the professional class, the establishment. Indian grunted his satisfaction. Groovy.

He looked after the disappearing sailboat. Indian was not a sailor, but it was obvious to him that the youth had gone too far out into the Channel. *I wonder if he did it to get laid?* Out there, all by yourself, take off your clothes and go — perhaps it was the girl that had wanted it that way. Complete isolation. Well, now they were paying for it. He laughed. *Sail on, sailor boy, with a cold cock.*

He was tired enough to sleep. He needed it. And he *would* need it. Once he started things rolling he would have to keep awake and keep it rolling. He would locate Cora and sack out. Yes. Cora. It would be a good release for him. Jeanne had been so damned careful once she became pregnant.

From behind him and below him he could hear two bands, first class and tourist; "The Sound of Music" from one, "We Shall Overcome" from the other. Voices, in a mixture of a half-dozen languages, singing the modern revolutionary's battle hymn, soothed him.

77

First: Get them together in some common cause.

Second: Get them listening to the outrages being heaped upon them — *and* their fellowman — and the demands for a better world.

Indian chuckled to himself. A feeling of pure power swelled through him. He stepped back from the railing and then reached out and touched it with his fingertips. He felt a throb, a vibration that ran through the whole vessel. "Go, ship, go, go," he said silently to himself.

Third: Write the petition and set up a committee to present the demands.

Fourth: Set up action squads. Mimeo machine for flyers. Radio room for communications. Let them keep the bridge and the engine room. They would do one of two things, either keep going, or turn around and go back. It did not matter to Indian at all. If the timing was right, he would need no more than two days . . .

Fifth: Lead them. That was the easy part. He remembered the coach. Just tell them what to do; and if everything else had been done correctly, they would do it.

The singing from below had stopped, as well as the handclapping. The rock beat was on now: the band had retired for the early evening, and now the records were being played. The Rolling Stones made

78

a heavy sullen sound that reminded him of a little boy he had once seen fighting with its mother. He thought about the speech he had made earlier. It had not been hard for Cora and Rome to mingle in the throng in the salon and start the handclapping and singing. Then he had made his speech. A straight anti-Vietnam, Ho-Ho-Ho pitch, using a lot of the themes and deliberately fuzzy thinking he had used on Cora and Ralph Rome earlier and with such success: a blend of Ho-Ho-Ho, draft resistance, the Blacks, SDS, Berkeley, and a primitive gut attack on Mayor Daley and the action freaks in Chicago. There were a lot of boos and disinterest, especially when he got into the Nonti Osorio *Dialogues* — but he had found what he was looking for. A solid core of malcontents who would be with him. He judged that core to be around a hundred and fifty. That gave him ten percent of the student passengers. Much more had been done with much less.

He sighed. Content. He turned below, passing a couple who were making love in one of the lifeboats. From ten feet away he could hear their heavy breathing and her whispered, "Go — go — go — *please —*"

Cora. He would find Cora and she would help him sleep.

79

3

And
You Walk Away from It
Without Psyche Pain...

CAPTAIN ABRAHAM COLDWATER, like a man who can remember every detail of a haunting nightmare, knew his ship and everything that had gone wrong in the forty-one months he had been aboard. His eye could catch dirt in the corner of a framed painting in one of the salons as easily as he could read the draft and deduce how much tonnage he had aboard. He was the first captain of the S.S. *New York* and he intended to ride her to the bone-yard or until he dropped dead from worry.

She was his possession. She was his reason for existence. He liked to read the inscription on a bronze plaque set below her nameplate on the weather bridge that stated the ideal:

The crossing on the S.S. New York *should be not merely a four-day passage but an adventure of memorable significance, never to be forgotten by man,*

woman or child. To have voyaged on this great ship
will be to have been cradled in and protected by
man's ultimate scientific and artistic achievements
in shipbuilding, and to have moved across the
cruelest body of water on earth in the capable care
of the finest seaman in the world, the American
Sailor.

Eustace Chamberlain
Designer-Builder

It was not uncommon for the chronically seasick
passenger, wandering around the great ship looking
for some relief, to discover this statement and with
lipstick or pencil add a reply in graphic language
suggesting what Mr. Chamberlain could do with his
ideal and his ship.

Coldwater stood naked before his basin. He
washed his shorts and T-shirt with easy thoroughness as he had done every day of his life at sea. It
was the first rule he had learned twenty-five years
before as an ordinary seaman: take it off and wash
it. When he was finished he draped the wet garments
over the towel rod and stepped into the shower. The
Peterson affair and the students were on his mind.

"Captain?" It was Stern, his steward.

"What the hell is it?"

"It's Mr. Chamberlain on the phone, sir. From
Palm Beach."

"Damn!" Coldwater grunted. "That man has, in

the forty-one months I've been aboard The Boat, called me from every part of the world and in every possible situation."

"Yes, sir."

Coldwater opened the shower door and glared at Stern. Soapsuds streamed down his thick legs. "He's called me when I was sitting on the can. Once when I was about to get in bed with a beautiful woman. When I was having dinner with a king and queen. And now it's complete, he's caught me washing my hocks!"

"Shall I have him call back, sir?"

"No, wait, *I'll* call *him*."

"Yes, sir."

"And get *his* ass out of bed for a change."

"Yes, sir. And sir —"

"What?"

"Sir Harry and Lady Weldon claim they have the Capriano Suite, but Miss Gloria Sheaffer refuses to move."

"I don't blame her," Coldwater said. "She's paying nearly three grand for the Capriano Suite, with a ten-month advance reservation. And *Sir* Harry and Lady Weldon had *no* reservations!"

"Yes, sir."

"All right. I'll take care of it. Where are they?"

"Chief Steward Bolten has them in the alcove —

starboard side — in the first-class lounge, popping his best champagne."

"Good man," Coldwater grunted. "Get back to the phone. Tell Eustace I'm busy and I'll call him back."

"And Dr. Jaca is here."

"Oh?" Coldwater looked puzzled. "Okay. Get hold of Chief Purser Alexs and have him meet me in the lounge. I want him with me for the Sir Harry business."

Coldwater rinsed off and hurried out of the bathroom. "Hello, Jaca."

"Captain —"

"Anything wrong?"

"Nothing serious. Mrs. George Bedford, first class. She had a heart history when she came aboard. I was informed about it. I've had to hospitalize her. She's under oxygen."

"Oh." Coldwater began to dress quickly, sailor style, socks and shoes first. "She need anything?"

"No, she has a private nurse."

"Okay, anything she needs. Tris! Tris Ramey!"

The door opened and a slim young man, Coldwater's secretary, carrying two dispatch cases. The secretary sat down, opened one case and took out a notebook. "Captain," he said quietly, pencil poised. Tris Ramey was ready.

"What's on for tonight?"

Coldwater was nearly finished with his dressing. He picked up the phone to the bridge. "Where are we?" he barked without identifying himself. He listened. "Okay, watch the glass. There's a suspected low out there — New York weather says something is building up. We should be getting it at about fifty west." He was not paying attention to Jaca, who had opened a black bag and taken out a syringe, and now approached him. Jaca made an injection into Coldwater's upper arm. He slammed the phone down.

"Ouch. What the hell was that?" Coldwater asked, rubbing his arm.

"B-12. You're a candidate for gout. Your last urine analysis showed a high uric acid imbalance."

"Meaning?"

"Good food, fine whiskey — a lot of both."

"Well, I have to live don't I?"

"Just be careful, Captain. You know the rules," Jaca said.

Coldwater looked at Tris Ramey. "Well?"

"Cocktails with Miss Sheaffer at seven-thirty; then your visit to the French Room before going to dinner, just in case there is someone aboard you might have missed."

"Yeah, yeah — what else?"

"Dinner; I have the seating plan."

"Add Sir Harry and Lady Weldon to my table — and of course Miss Sheaffer — fine woman, Jaca."

Jaca hesitated. "I know," he said quietly. "I've been invited also."

Coldwater looked up sharply. "You know her?"

"Casual friends."

Coldwater squinted. "Well — well — small world." Coldwater sighed. "Good! She always has an interesting crowd. If there's anybody aboard that has anything, Miss Sheaffer will find them out." Coldwater continued to dress. He glanced at Tris Ramey. "Anything else?"

"Cocktails, French Room, dinner, private party with Mr. and Mrs. Bannerman."

Coldwater wrinkled his nose. "I don't like that one. I'm going to hit the sack early tonight. That Colonel Peterson business has made it a very nasty day."

Tris Ramey made a note. "Very well, sir."

"Send the Bannermans a nice note. My personal stationery. Say, ah, let me see —" Coldwater threw his head back and began to think.

Jaca picked up his bag and started out.

"Hold it, Jaca, just a minute," Coldwater said. "Just tell them the usual — duty on the bridge — and send them a bottle of Dom Perignon."

"Yes, sir."

"And bright and early tomorrow morning, Tris, we get through the mail. It's piling up. I don't like to get too far behind from one trip to another, or I forget who the hell I'm writing to."

88

"I know, sir." Tris Ramey smiled. He nodded to Jaca and slipped out of the room as quietly as he had entered.

"Want a drink?" Coldwater asked Jaca when the two men were alone.

"I don't think so, Captain."

"Jaca, what about that Peterson girl?"

"She's still out."

"Jesus. Sixteen hundred of them. God knows how many of them have cases of the clap and hepatitis; watch for that, Jaca. If they brought it aboard, caught in some quick thrust during their European summer, that's all right; but I wouldn't want it spread around."

"There isn't a hell of a lot I can do about it."

"I know, I know, they're like a rabbit hutch down there. Jesus! Sixteen hundred of them!" Coldwater returned abruptly and picked up the phone. "Tris, get a list of every empty cabin, in all classes, especially tourist." Coldwater dropped the phone. "Couple of stewards last year at this time were letting them have empties for private parties."

"I've heard."

"That poor man," Coldwater said, standing and putting the finishing touches to his tie and cuffs. "Well, too bad. He told me his wife died and he was off to the wars, left the girl with his sister, in Paris.

But that kid, the one who looks like an Indian, he was a cool sonofabitch, wasn't he?"

"Very cool," Jaca said.

"Luis, how long you been aboard The Boat?"

"Two and a half years, now, sir, why?"

"Then you know what it's all about."

"I think so, sir."

"Twenty-five hundred on the lists and one thousand in crew. And I'm their God and Master — it's more people, *every week,* under my direct authority than most generals ever get in a lifetime. And I have the same absolute control that Ahab did. We're all Ahabs, actually, although no one who has never gone to sea can understand it. We're the last of the total Gods; and I feel it, Luis, I want you to know, I feel it, especially when I see something like today with Colonel Peterson —"

Jaca listened to the man, who was not much older than himself; and he felt the responsibility himself, only a small edge of it, but it was there. Jaca was aware that even he, who held life and death in his hands, depended on the man standing before him to get him safely from shore to shore.

The door opened. "Captain — Sir Harry — sir?" Stern stood there.

"Yeah — yeah — coming." Stern disappeared. Coldwater picked up his hat. "I don't know what got me going, Jaca. That Peterson business, I guess."

"Get some rest this trip, Captain," Jaca said. "Not only as your doctor but as Luis, all right, Abe?"

"All right, Luis." Captain Coldwater strode out of the room, fit and trim, master of the finest ship ever built, and alert, still alert to the sea.

It was a magnificent night. The great ship moved through the dark seas ablaze with lights, looking like a lawn Christmas tree that someone had forgotten to turn out, surrounded by a glow of joy and peace. And Coldwater knew exactly how to use that aura. The captain of the S.S. *New York* possessed both tact and a certain talent for getting people to do what he wanted.

Sir Harry Weldon had walked to the railing with Captain Coldwater, both of them sipping champagne, and allowed himself to be seduced in that starry night.

More champagne was served to the Knight. Within a few minutes Coldwater had gotten down to business. He assured Sir Harry that the less spacious Arcadia Suite they were presently in was more than equal in luxury to the Capriano. Then he added what was already known and obvious: "And the Capriano Suite was occupied when you came aboard, Sir Harry."

"Quite." The one word was frosted and very, very

cold; but it was over. After a decent interval they returned to Lady Weldon.

"He just wanted me to hold his hand," Coldwater explained to the purser when it was over. They made their way through the confusion of the first-class lounge. There were a great many students. "What the hell are they doing up here?" Coldwater demanded.

"A few of them are traveling first class," Alexs explained.

Something drew Coldwater's attention to one side as they stepped out onto the boatdeck. "Mister, I think you'd better investigate that lifeboat. Only don't be shocked at what you find."

Alexs looked around. "A stowaway, Captain?"

Coldwater set his teeth on edge. "No, it isn't a stowaway. It's a boy and girl under the lifeboat cover. And they aren't praying. And they aren't reading the Koran, either."

"Yes, sir," Alexs said grimly. "Where will they go next?"

"You ask that question, Mister, because you and I are not so young anymore. I remember a rainy night in Shanghai, in a rickshaw —"

"Sir?"

"Never mind," Coldwater said, motioning toward the lifeboat. "See to it — no, belay that. Let 'em

alone. Just have the deck crew check the boats every
fifteen minutes."

At seven-thirty Jaca finished the last of the paper-
work for the ship's records on Elienne Peterson. He
hesitated about going to Gloria Sheaffer's cocktail
party, but decided that he *would* like to see her again
and have a couple of drinks before dinner in company rather than alone. He went into the hospital to
check on Mrs. Bedford and Elienne Peterson.

The girl was sleeping quietly. He turned to the old
woman. "How do you do," Jaca said as he approached the bed. "I'm Dr. Jaca." He automatically
reached for the pulse. Stronger. Not strong, but
stronger. Jaca felt depressed, watching the frail little
woman's eyes follow him and his movements.

"How do you do, Dr. Jaca. Thank you for taking
care of me."

"How do you feel?"

"Unwilling."

"About what?"

"Everything. Unwilling to die. Unwilling to live.
Unwilling to go through the next four days."

"We usually have good crossings this time of
the year."

"Dr. Jaca, I've been crossing this ocean since I was

93

seven years old. I know what it can do. Without warning."

"I'll speak to the captain."

"Don't bother Abe Coldwater for me," Mrs. Bedford said, a twinkle in her eye. "Talk to God, if you have influence there."

"None whatsoever," Jaca said. "Is there anything you want?"

"Nothing, thank you," Mrs. Bedford said. "But come back tomorrow and maybe I'll tell you the story of my life. You remind me of a lover I once had. He was dark and handsome and sensitive like you. I had three lovers at once, during my first trip to Europe alone. In Rome. Before the First World War. My mama thought I was studying music. And I was. My! How they could sing. They would come to my villa, walking up that sunny winding road, singing, sweep me off my feet and take me to bed. Morning, Afternoon and Night! That's what I called them. My God, they were beautiful! With such round arms!"

Jaca laughed out loud. Nurse Claudet glanced up from her book, a look of pained disapproval in her eye. Jaca patted Mrs. Bedford's hand: a delicate hand with a skin like parchment paper, cold to his touch. "I'll be coming back for details."

"Ha!" Mrs. Bedford breathed deeply and smiled. "I never could trust a man who didn't have a healthy prurient curiosity."

"Good night — rest." He motioned Nurse Claudet to one side. "You will be relieved at midnight, Nurse."

"Can you imagine! At her age, nearly dead, thinking about lovers when she would be better off making her peace with God."

"Are you French?" Jaca asked. "French, Catholic?"

"Yes, of course."

"You're right," Jaca said, scribbling instructions for a mild sedative. "I'm sure she's hallucinating."

"Yes, of course, that's it."

"Good night, Nurse Claudet." He handed her the instructions and walked away.

At seven o'clock, before the arrival of her guests, Gloria Sheaffer was putting the finishing touches on the placement of the hors d'oeuvres and the bar. The champagne was chilled, the scotch, bourbon, vodka, mixers and glasses arranged. Several vases of flowers decorated the room. Two stewards stood nearby as the final decisions were made. A gallon of very dry martinis had been mixed and now rested in the freezer. All was ready. Satisfied, she retired to her bedroom to dress.

She stood before her mirror and gazed at her body. Yes, still there, but how much longer, Gloria? And for what?

And for whom?

She began to apply the finishing touches to her

face. She heard something crash in the sitting room: a glass, she decided. It reminded her of the scuffle in the French Room that afternoon. How long ago was it that she had done the same things? It was more than fifteen years ago, she heard herself reply.

They have Johnson and Nixon. We had Ike and Kennedy. Only we weren't consciously anti-anything. Boredom? Yes, antiboredom. We were very conscious of that.

There had been a party in the East Sixties in New York and everyone had gone to P.J.'s for a last drink. Someone mentioned the new jets — the 707's. *I'll race you around the world!*

"You go east, we'll go west!"

"The first one back to P.J.'s wins!"

They had not even gone home to change. Two groups of them. Five days without sleep. She had worn her ball gown the entire time. Children at play in the whole world with no one to call them inside when it grew dark. The students she had seen in the French Room were no different. Less style, perhaps; no, *different* styles. Perhaps her peer group had a slight edge in one area, that of the bath.

She chose the gold gown. The one that gave her bosom the most exposure, yet was quite acceptable.

Suddenly she was confused and did not know why. It *mattered*. She did not know why, but it mattered seeing the new generation kicking up a fuss. There had been so few things in her life that mattered. She was pleased, even picked up, by the idea of something being important enough to matter.

Ralph Rome was not feeling so groovy at seven-thirty. He was in a down syndrome; he either had to pick up on another joint of marijuana or suffer the drop and have the heavies fall over him. He sat at his table in the tourist dining room and stared unhappily at the cube steak under its thick gumbo sauce, the smear of mashed potatoes and the singularly tired string beans. He took one mouthful of each, then shoved the plate away.

The girl on his left was pretty enough, but she had a network of fine scars over her face; probably from some childhood accident, Rome thought. He thought of her as ugly. The girl on his right was unable to shut up. She was very tall, nearly six feet, dark, and wagging her jawbone about Astrology. The youth opposite him was fat and neat. He wore glasses and talked his thing, which was Middle English Politics, whenever the girl with the big mouth gave him a chance; he reminded Rome of a fat cat.

Rome really *wanted* another joint. He looked at the three of them. Why not? he thought, trying to provoke himself out of his down funk. I'll turn 'em on. Right here. Now. I'll do it. He broke into the middle of one of Big Mouth's comments about the age of Aquarius.

"Listen, have you heard what they're actually *doing?*"

Fat Cat opposite him (Taurus, Earth) did not miss a beat with his fork. Ugly flicked her eyes, glanced at him hopefully, dropped her eyes and stirred her mashed potatoes like a good Capricorn full of mental fears should. And Big Mouth (Aquarius, aggressive) paused long enough to chew, which gave Rome his opening.

"We pay the price, right? I mean, look at this slop — I don't know if it's steak or somebody's gizzard they carved up."

They were listening. He started all over again. Taking it slowly, easing into it. Once he had them, he settled back in his chair and began to include surrounding tables. In ten minutes he had an open dialogue going on among five tables. He smiled inwardly.

At precisely seven-thirty that evening, Colonel Algernon Peterson, wearing a suit of tweeds for the first time in years, stood at the entrance of the first-class dining room and surveyed the huge salon. He felt soothed. There were nice people here. Very nice.

The retired and the elderly; the comfortable and even the rich; many proud possessors of one thousand shares of General Motors or Du Pont; the solid, secure citizens of mother earth; the unpretentious yet firm rulers of the world. In every country he had ever visited, Colonel Peterson had found these to be his people. There was no betraying of confidences here. When a man gave his word, you could put it in the bank and draw cash on it. He was soothed and pleased. The gray-haired men and women, the few thickening faces with carefully preserved back teeth on which they hung their bridges, the carefully selected, expensive rack dresses and rack suits: all of it was home to him.

The clatter of silver and glass and the murmur of conversation in a dozen languages blotted from his mind his most immediate rancor over his daughter's situation. There was the deeper wound which he knew would never be wiped away. But for the moment, he was almost peaceful. What was done was done, never mind the reasons why. Somehow, he would cope. He nodded to the maître d'. He managed a smile. "Good evening. Colonel Peterson."

"Good evening, Colonel." The maître d' began to examine his lists.

But the maître d' did not have him on the first-class lists: there had been an oversight in making the dining room seating arrangements. It would be an hour before Colonel Peterson would be seated. And in that time his rage would slide upward like an exponential curve with each passing minute. In the end he would dine utterly alone.

"It's seven-thirty, m'dear," Lady Weldon said to her Knight.

Sir Harry struggled with his cuff links. He was in a rage over what had happened to him since he had come aboard the S.S. *New York*. "Who is this person — Gloria Sheaffer — probably some American beefsteak heiress. Do you understand, my dear, just look what she has made us. We are *here!* We are in the Arcadia Suite and *she* is in the Capriano Suite — please, would you bloody well mind helping me with this bloody naughty link — and *Sheaffer,* whom you insist we have cocktails with — and which you accepted without telling me — sounds *Jewish* — I think it's bloody cheek!"

Lady Weldon slipped the pins of the cuff links easily. She caressed his freshly shaved chin. She smiled. She remained silent. She knew her Knight. She loved him, but he could be so terribly dull and stuffy at times. Male vanity, coupled with snobbism, was a terrible burden; and for Lady Weldon, the only real weakness a man could have was to indulge in such pettiness.

"*Must* we go, now really, m'dear? *Must* we?" Sir Harry demanded.

"Captain Coldwater is being very nice. It was his invitation to the cocktail party and then to dine at his table —" She said no more. She knew very well that he would have been insufferable if he had *not* been invited. She sighed. It would be very nice to be with new people for a little while.

At seven-thirty the first guests arrived at Gloria's cocktail party. Within ten minutes three-quarters of those expected had arrived, and babbling happily they pressed around Captain Coldwater.

Captain Coldwater, plainly enjoying himself, smiled down at Gloria Sheaffer's bosom. He stood in the middle of the sitting room, a bourbon and water in his hand, and played his favorite role: the wise and sophisticated sailor with deep blue eyes that had seen it all. He was resplendent in his whites and gold braid and smelled strongly of a brisk cologne. He was polite, he was courtly, witty, diplomatic. Second Officer Joe Trapp slipped into the room escorting a handsome couple. The captain watched them for a moment and satisfied himself that Trapp was on the

make for the wife. The husband, a tall, sickly-looking
fellow with a beard and a string of love beads, did
not look like much competition. Coldwater made a
mental note to put a damper on Trapp's social activities. The woman was beautiful, though; no, not
beautiful, handsome. And probably rich. Captain
Coldwater turned back to Gloria Sheaffer and feasted
his eyes on her bosom, enjoying a pleasant sensation
of lust.

By the time Jaca arrived, the rooms were so
crowded he did not have a chance to speak to Gloria.
But they spotted each other. Gloria Sheaffer spoke
soundlessly across the crowded room, mouthing the
words. "Call me —"

Jaca nodded and smiled. The party moved,
swirled. Time, here, was different from the time in
the French Room. Gloria had been very careful about
her guests. She had spent two hours going over the
passenger lists that afternoon, putting an x beside
the names of those she didn't know but would make
a point of meeting during the voyage, and circling
the names of those she knew, most of whom were
now there. She moved effortlessly through the crowd,
born to it, commanding. There were Lulu Tennington and that creepy photographer husband of hers,
with young Officer Trapp. Interesting. The laughter
here was not merely laughter, but careful tonalities;

this was not, after all, the French Room and a mating game, or the students' open game of stud; this was big money play. Partners might be exchanged, surely, but there were considerations. Money and power. A woman may shed her mate, but *not* her money. A man may shed his mate, but not his image *or* his money. The process of casting off and adding on did involve something of a blunt instrument approach and tended to leave the losers bloodied and sprawling. But somehow it was all handled with a finesse, a superior tact, like a gentlemanly game of chess; when one was checkmated, it was usually quick and to the point, with someone saying, "I'm getting a divorce. My lawyers will be in touch."

By seven-thirty that evening, Cora Ingersoll was about to give up on Indian. She had recognized his type, but she was as easily drawn to action freaks as a meth monster rolls his dollar bill and sniffs out. She sat alone and quiet at the first sitting (obeying Indian's instructions to stay out of sight and not talk to anyone) and poked at her mashed potatoes. She had two offers while she fussed over her dinner. One from a very handsome Chinese student with a fan of black hair to his shoulders that shone and made him look like a Hong Kong mini–doll; and one from a brainy type who stuttered and was a *cinéma-vérité* film maker. He wore his viewfinder like a love medallion and was constantly finding things to frame, squinting and squatting and making angles.

But she waited for Indian. There was a lot she knew about him already. His eyes were too bright, and at times they seemed to recede into his thin face. He talked a lot of gut. And like many other action bang-ons, he was very good with his reactions and he would, she was sure, use anything to win. It made no difference to her that she had been wasted by action freaks before. There would come a connection, she was sure. Perhaps it would be Indian and perhaps not. Taking over the ship was a pretty enlarged way to get through a dull four-day crossing, however, and since action bang-ons were her special bag, she decided to cool it and see what Indian would come up with. She was not looking for a *hang-up*, she assured herself, but a *connection*. Then with the connection, feel it out, see what it was all about, and listen to the presences. Wait for the vibrations, Cora. And why not?

She stirred her mashed potatoes until they were taken away by a waiter not much older than herself, who made a suggestive remark to her. When at last she looked up, there was Indian.

He motioned to her.

"Let's groove," Indian said. "There's something going on in G-420. It's for singles. You know, like there are a lot of singles that can't make a connection, so they all gang up in one cabin, you know?"

When Cora did not say anything, he looked down at her. "You want to take a look?"

Cora shrugged.

They moved through the ebb and flow of bodies in the companionways and the common rooms and made their way past his cabin and pressed on, moving into a quieter section of the ship.

"Is that it?" Cora said.

Before them was a pile of clothing. Shoes, jackets, shirts, slips, bras, shorts, socks, sandals, panties and dresses were scattered around in front of G-420. "You ever been in one before?" Indian asked.

"No." Cora shivered. "But — I have an idea."

"You take your clothes off, leave them here, and go in. It'll be dark. It doesn't make any difference what you do, or to whom —"

"You want something a little more refined?" Cora asked.

"Are you asking, or begging?" Indian replied.

"Personal. How's that? Personal, is that okay?" Cora flared.

Indian chuckled scornfully. "You want to groove, or you want to start a hang-up?"

Cora Ingersoll shivered again. "Groove," she said. "But not in there. Not like that."

"Afraid?"

"No."

"Want to take a look?"

"I told you I don't like to look. I have my fantasies."

"That's right, you did."

"But *you* want to go in, don't you?" Cora said suddenly.

"I've got a lot of action in front of me, baby. I need to relax. I need to turn on —"

"I'll accomplish that," Cora said.

Several singles came up. They stripped silently, and nude they entered G-420. Cora got a brief glance inside. There was a solid mass of nude flesh, bodies in every attitude and position. Naked bodies moved in a kind of ghostly slow motion. She saw boys and girls, boys with boys and girls with girls. The door closed.

She took Indian by the hand and led him away. He gave a little derisive laugh. "It's a nice way, baby, if you can't make a connection. Would you deny them their bag? I mean, they've got to do *something* besides take cold showers, you know? It's a nice way. Nobody knows and nobody cares. And you walk away from it without psyche pain and hang-ups that might get in the way of a man's thing. You got this tension, see, and you go in, and there it is — release."

They were at Cora's cabin. She entered, turned on the light, made sure the cabin was empty, and turned out the light. She locked the door. "You want to groove, we'll groove," she said in the dark as she reached for him. "But it's me. It's not the whole world."

"It's all so existential, baby, you know?"

"No," she said. "No, it isn't. Somehow it isn't."

He thought abruptly of Jeanne, waiting in Paris, waiting for him, with his child. Then she was gone, dismissed from his mind forever, and he turned hungrily to Cora's giving mouth.

At seven-thirty the great ship moved over the deep with the authority and majesty of an impatient monarch. It was going full speed toward home. The bands played, people drank, people strolled the decks, people made love, relaxed, secure, on their way to the land of giants. And in the second-class lounge the gray and starched and polite were lining up to get into the theater for *The Secret of Dongo Canyon* starring John Wayne.

4

What's the Action...?

HE AWOKE at 4 A.M. Cora was asleep, still nestled in his arms. He held one of her breasts in his palm. She had one leg thrown over his body. It was cool. The sibilant hiss of the air conditioner was something apart from the general hum of the ship's engines, which he could actually hear now for the first time. The ship rolled gently. Cora lay back and then was thrown gently back into his arms. The vibration, which he remembered feeling the evening before on the deck, was stronger here: he was deeper in the bowels of the ship.

He got out of bed carefully, easing away from the slim and beautiful girl, who stirred, rolled over and pulled up a blanket.

Indian dressed quickly. His instinct told him the time was now. Get to them while they were still asleep after their first night's drunk. Hit them and hit

111

them hard. He made his plans as he slipped down the companionways to his own cabin.

"Rome!" he said in a fierce undertone. "Rome — f'chrissake!" He ignored the nude girl in the opposite — his — bunk.

"What — what — what the hell!"

"Shussh!"

"Indian! Where the hell you been?"

"Shut up and get dressed, we got work to do."

"What time is it?" Rome scrunched around and snapped on the bedlight. "Jesus, it's four o'clock in the *morning!*"

"You want action, the time is *now,*" Indian said.

"But how?" Rome was coming awake.

"Meet me on the starboard boat deck in five minutes. Don't be late."

"But —"

Indian slipped out of the door.

On the boat deck, Indian leaned on the railing and studied the gray dawn. The wind whipped at his hair. He smoked one cigarette after another. He thought and thought and analyzed and formulated and planned.

Ralph Rome's chunky figure materialized out of the darkness and joined him at the railing. "I'm cold —"

"How many did you guess applauded me when I

grabbed the mike last night and made that Ho-Ho-Ho speech?"

"Why?"

"How *many?*"

"One hundred fifty; maybe more," Rome said. "There were also a lot of boos."

"That was to be expected," Indian said. "First day aboard the ship and everybody is looking for a connection, right?"

"Right."

"So, they didn't want to hear any drag."

"So?"

"Now they've *made* their connections," Indian said. "They'll be waking up, going to breakfast, taking a second look at the guy they slept with — and at her — and their eyes will start wandering —"

"That's pretty good," Rome said. He hunched himself against the stiff breeze. "S'what?"

"They've made their connections, so now we take their minds off their good times, and turn them on, gently, to something else. We establish ourselves. We establish a *thing,* you dig? And we watch which ones become part of it and which ones do not. The ones that stand up, who are looking for action, those are the ones we put into our cadre."

"Jesus," Rome breathed, genuinely respectful. "That's groovy, Chief —"

"Shut up, and you know how we do it?"

"You want me to ask, or shut up?" Rome said.

"Come'n, don't be smart-assed," Indian said sarcastically. "This is something, man. A *stroke* —"

"All right, go —"

"How many can you depend on for the first sitting at breakfast?"

"For what?"

"To do as we do — *not*," Indian emphasized, turning and jabbing a finger into Rome's chest, "as we *say* do. But just follow the leader?"

"Oh, you mean —"

"Hardheads," Indian said. "The fuck-ups. The hoods. The leather-jacket set. How many will pick up on an improvisation?"

"At the first sitting?"

"The first sitting," Indian emphasized. "It's gotta be the first."

"Not many will be up to eat, you know."

"How *many*?"

"Maybe fifty. And there are some pretty heavy guys aboard. There's a bike party scene, I think they're from the Midwest. They did the whole Euroscene with their chicks and they're pretty up tight. You must have seen them; they're doing the whole thing; muscle. And they *like* to eat."

"I've seen a few of them. Good. You know where they sack in?"

114

"I can find out."

"Find out. That's number one. Now, number two. Anybody else you can think of that will follow the leader, get them up too."

"What's the action?"

"We're going to stage a demonstration over the lousy food at the first sitting. I'll start it, then you get *everybody* out of their sacks with the call to action."

"I don't follow —"

"I'll spell it out for you. We get a hundred people at the first sitting, more or less, right?"

"I didn't say a hundred, but it's a pretty good idea."

"The food is lousy, we start complaining and sending the eggs back. The stewards and waiters start to growl. We growl back. I throw an egg plate at one of them. Then everyone starts throwing eggs and salt shakers — and we have an action scene with the waiters and stewards, right?"

"Go." Ralph Rome rubbed his hands together. "I'm with you."

"That's when I need some goons like the hoodies, and other types to help me start that first action. *Then,* before it is even turned on, you run and wake everybody — yelling fire! Get it?"

"But will they come?"

"They'll come," Indian said confidently.

"Got it. What's next?"

"Why, they'll send in the Marines, won't they?

Why, man, they'll have to. There will be a few
fistfights, a few busted heads and broken noses, a
few cuts and bruises, but by then we'll have our
issue."

"*Not,*" Ralph Rome moaned, holding his head,
"*brutality* again. Jesus, that's been worn so thin after
Daley's Chicago scene, nobody believes that anymore."

"Brutality is only a phony issue, a side bar. No, a
list of demands. Lousy medical attention, lousy food,
suppression of rights. You see, out of this action, we
will have blooded some of the cats, right?"

"Right. A busted nose is good sentiment."

" 'Kay. So out of the busted noses and the hurt
arms and the hysterical emotions, we build the core
of our cadres. We'll set up committees and become
the elite. Everyone else will be *ass aching* to get into
it with us."

"We'll be exclusive." Rome nodded, agreeing, feeling it. The thrill of being a partisan welled up in him.
"Where do I come in?"

"You're my Number One. I give the word, and you
give it to them. You spread it around." Indian turned
and put his arm around Rome's shoulder. "You're my
numero uno —"

"Watch it," Rome said. "Look who's out for a
stroll."

They watched as Colonel Peterson, his head down, chin buried in the folds of his greatcoat, strode in the damp and silent early morning. He glanced up briefly at the two youths at the railing, then recognized them. He paused.

"Good morning," he said quietly.

"Good morning," Indian said.

"Why?" Colonel Peterson asked softly, staring at them.

"It's a whole new scene, Colonel," Indian said easily. "Don't try to understand it." He smiled. "Even Caesar woke up with a hangover."

"But I've had to understand things all my life."

"That's your hang-up. Now it's wide open."

"Who said so?" Colonel Peterson said. "Why are there no credits for my values?"

"Because you blew it, Colonel. You hung on too long to the wrong things. You didn't improve things one inch. Wrong, Colonel. Wrong."

"Who said they were wrong?"

"Time, Colonel. Just time."

"I'm too tired and old, is that it?"

"Old, perhaps. Tired, no." Indian made a visible show of feeling his ears and nose. He smiled, his most charming smile.

"Did I injure you? Seriously?" Colonel Peterson asked.

"No," Indian said. "No, Colonel. I'm young and bounce back rather easily."

"Is time the answer?" Colonel Peterson asked.

"It is an answer, Colonel, but actually it isn't. If you want it straight and groovy?"

"I want it straight and groovy," Colonel Peterson said. "I've got a young girl down there. I've got to try and understand her."

"I'm sorry about that," Indian said. "But time isn't the answer either. It's a concept — of the waste of life."

"Is that the new, flat abstraction? No waste of life."

"I'm not being personal, Colonel," Indian said easily, "I mean about your being a professional killer — I mean, soldier. But if you can understand that, then you're hip, Colonel. That's it."

"No, no," Colonel Peterson said, turning away, "I'm not hip. But thank you anyway." He moved off down the deck.

"I thought he was going to start in again," Rome said.

"No, not him," Indian replied thoughtfully. "You see, once you get to their gut, and it's very hard to *find* their guts, then you find shitheads underneath."

"But," Rome injected tentatively, "he talked, he

118

sounded like, you know, he wanted to know how to handle his daughter."

"If he had the chance," Indian said coldly, "he would do anything to have things just the way they were before he found out his daughter was an acid head and a sex freak." Indian lit a cigarette. He watched the solitary figure on the deck, far down at the other end of the ship. "Anything, man. Anything to have his neat world, his neat daughter, his neat dreams, his neat and tidy morality back the way they were before. He doesn't care about his daughter. He cares only about being faced with the fact that there is something his values won't or can't allow him to cope with, and overcome. He's face to face with a kind of reality he never suspected existed, for the first time in his life. And you know what? You know how he's tried to handle it?"

"How?" Rome asked huskily, not really wanting to know.

"First, violence. He slammed into me — us, like a fifty-ton tank. That didn't work, so he made his appeal to Captain Coldwater, which is a return to the establishment for support, old buddies, you know, and failing that, now, *now* he stalks the decks of a lonely ship burying himself in self-pity." Indian laughed scornfully.

"Let's go and get this mixer working," he said.

At seven-forty-five, as the ship's log would note later, there was a disturbance in the tourist dining room.

They hit like a shrapnel grenade.

On the left side of the dining room, aloof from the run of regular students, the Midwestern bike club and their chicks ate healthy breakfasts and talked about their kicks riding "those heavy hills in Austria." On the right — and scattered thinly through the rest of the huge dining room — were the students. As many as Rome and Indian and Cora could get to come to breakfast. Fat Cat was there, and Ugly and Big Mouth; the Chinese student wearing a Honolulu shirt and jockey shorts; the film maker was there, with a 16-mm Bolex which he kept adjusting, playing with the focus and checking the light. And Rome and Cora and Indian. Fifty or sixty others were scattered around. They were served by the usual ill-tempered waiters who loathed and despised the indulged students. Mostly they were young Puerto Ricans and a few young Blacks and whites, as well as a sprinkle of old-timers who resented being in tourist when their talents would bring large tips in first class.

The eggs kept being returned. Once, twice, three times. The potbellied little fry cook came out of the swing door and took a look at the students, glared at them, cursed them, but returned to the galley and to slamming his frypans around.

Then Cora stuck her finger down her throat and made a sound like vomiting. Then Ugly did the same thing. Then Fat Cat actually *did* vomit — then Indian, who winked at Fat Cat admiringly.

The waiters, who saw none of the action, just the results, stood around and shifted uneasily from one foot to another, silent and amazed. Then the fry cook came out again, not so hot this time, and looked at the sick students. He shook his head. Those frypans were the finest in the world. He salt-stoned them every night and removed them from the galley and took them to his fo'c'sle — it *had* to be the eggs. A bad crate; those goddamn greedy French; selling bad eggs!

Indian gave Ralph Rome a signal and his *numero uno* slipped out and knocked on nearly every door on G Deck, screaming the alarm. Indian had phrased it very carefully, and even had Rome repeat it several times. *"The pigs are beating up on our people! The pigs are beating up on our people!"*

In the dining room the potbellied little fry cook started over to the students to apologize when he was hit smack in the middle of the forehead with a mustard bottle and fell poleaxed to the deck. The waiters avenged him. The students struck back. Dishes, chairs, bottles, plates, knives and forks sailed through the air.

Ralph Rome's alarm brought an immediate response. The students came — dressed, half-dressed and nearly nude — and crowded into the dining room. The battle had aligned itself on two sides of the dining room: the waiters, cooks and a few deck sailors on one side, the students, reinforced by the bike club with their leather pants and jackets, on the other. In less than fifteen minutes the dining room was a shambles. Screams and oaths filled the air. Individual fistfights broke out, mostly between the bike crowd and the crew. There were a lot of cuts and bruises and a few broken noses and fingers, but no real damage. It came to a stalemate, with both sides milling around and shouting oaths and curses at each other, accusing each other of starting the fight or serving lousy rotten food, or both. This did not last long, because the deck crew came in with fire hoses and washed the students back out of the dining room, and then pressed on, driving them back to their cabins. A few students got trapped and were unmercifully hosed down with the high-pressure water by enthusiastic sailors and a few waiters who had joined them; but generally there was a lot of laughing and horseplay, and even the crew got into the spirit of the battle after a while, when several students grabbed fire hoses of their own and it degenerated into a water fight, which pleased Indian very much.

Throughout the whole time he and Cora and Rome and Ugly had skirted the edges of the fight observing faces and catching a name when they could and jotting it all down for future reference. It did not last long. It couldn't. There was no direction to the student rebellion, but Indian felt confident that he could take care of that.

They retired to their cabin and laughed and talked, and Ugly proved her depth and character when it was discovered she had broken her index finger and had not mentioned it.

Like the scuffle in the French Room, the student rebellion over the eggs was discussed by first- and second-class passengers, joked about, laughed at, and eventually forgotten, no one taking it more seriously than a panty raid or a football rally fight. The rest of the day was quiet. The lower decks were patrolled and the captain made a speech to the packed student luncheon assembly, in which he stated that he appreciated good fun like anyone else, and the eggs were being investigated and the responsible people would be dealt with. He ended by saying that if it happened again, the entire deck would be confined to cabins.

There were a few leftover individual fights, when students who had been roughed up unnecessarily by the crew with the hoses found they could not contain their fury. The whole affair was quite forgotten by three that afternoon when the social director arranged a tug-o'-war between groups of students and wisely, at Coldwater's instructions, opened the bar — but served only beer. Many first- and second-class passengers, already bored with their voyage, stood on the upper decks and watched the tug-o'-war and cheered; a few hustlers made winning bets on the outcome; and bottles were sneaked from first class down to the students, and it was good fun and the sun was shining; and in G-703 Indian had organized his resistance committee.

The core would be the Action Council, of which he was council chairman.

First on the order of business would be the drafting of a resolution for a Petition for Redress.

The bike group would be security, which they liked.

Rome would be executive secretary, which he liked.

Cora would be recording secretary, which she liked.

Ugly would be student intercommunications with foreign students because she spoke five languages, which she liked.

Big Mouth would be in charge of cultural relations (Astrology) within the group, which she liked.

Fat Cat was in charge of practices, precedence and theory, which he liked.

Film Maker was in charge of recorded history, which he liked.

Ling Jung was ambassador extraordinary liaison with the ship's commanders, which he liked. (He had learned to use his inscrutability.)

Within this executive council there were heads of action groups. Mimeoed flyers. Radio Room. Intra-ship communications. Internal and external security.

By five that afternoon, there was aboard the S.S. *New York* a functioning, highly intelligent agency prepared to take the ship over, and no one knew any-thing about it.

But Luis Jaca suspected. He had spent the whole day making dressings for the wounded and the cut and bruised. He had listened to them as they paraded before him with their busted heads and their arro-gance, intelligence and demands, and he knew. There was one figure with no name that continually emerged. He recognized it by their offhand remarks and comments. Indian. In a dozen different ways, it was Indian.

He worked and he thought and he reflected and it all came up Indian.

"Take over, Carol," Jaca said. He glanced at the few remaining students in line, ignoring them, and walked out. He wanted a drink. He wanted to think. It was all coming back and he didn't think he could handle it. He wanted to rest. He was an old revolutionary and he had no victories. And he knew what was happening. He smelled it.

5

War as Pure as Gettysburg —Iwo Jima...

FOREMOST in Indian's mind now that the Action Council was organized and the election of officers and committee heads was completed, was that the machinery, the structure of the North Atlantic Students Redress Assembly (NASRA) must be able to go on functioning after he had been taken in for questioning or even arrest. That he be questioned, or even arrested, was a vital part of his overall plan. Once he had the faith and trust of the students, once the *issue* had become a gut problem for all of his following, once he had proved that he was worthy of their trust and that he was one of them, then the guaranteed trigger to set the entire ship aflame with rebellion would be his arrest by Coldwater. It was, however, necessary that his arrest be based *on the issue*.

The atmosphere in G-703 was charged. They were

inscribing their Petition of Redress. There was genuine spirit among the students. They shared everything. One of the bike group lit a joint of pot, and
after a few drags passed it around. A girl from Ben-
nington held the head of a seasick boy from the West
Coast and kept moving back and forth to the john for
cold towels. They were *together*. They were *sharing*.
They were participating in the very things that the
outside, adult world denied them. They were themselves. They were *now*. They were the existential,
pragmatic Love Others. They discussed everything
from the resistance of the Catholic Church to the
Pill, to Senator McCarthy, Vietnam, SDS, Draft Resistance, Nixon, the Rolling Stones, the Blacks. They
sang "We Shall Overcome." They listened while a
young boy, by far the youngest in the group, read a
passage from *Ramparts* magazine and spoke elo-
quently on the oppression of the Puerto Rican and
Black waiters in the tourist dining room. They applauded when one of the bike group turned on, admitting in halting inarticulate language that was
fuzzy from too much pot, that he didn't really ". . .
understand, but I know I can't live with this shit
anymore, or go back to Alpaca, Nebraska . . ." and
he would do whatever the executive committee of the
Action Council asked of him. His chick, a lovely little
girl in a leather mini-skirt and jacket, gave him a big
love kiss right on the mouth for that.

Now and then Indian, lazing back, refusing a drag on a passing stick, his eyes and ears alert for anything that would add to his design, would rap the deck with an empty cognac bottle and call for a return to the point.

"I think we should continue, and get this thing *nailed down,* you know? I mean, we haven't even got through the preamble and everybody is beginning to hang loose as if it were all wrapped up. Listen, now, this is a heavy bag we've got here. If we want to accomplish anything at all, you know, we gotta get down to it. All right, how do we address ourselves to the preamble?"

Ugly held up her hand. Indian gave her a nod. She straightened her skirt. "Well, I think we have to focus, you know? Focus on what it's all about?" She looked around, hopefully, for help. "I mean, they busted several of the kids pretty bad. There was a whole stream of us going up to the doctor —"

There was a lot of yeahing and yessing and general agreement that Ugly had made a good point. Indian rapped the cognac bottle.

"How many of you went up for medical attention?" Indian asked, driving in coldly above the noise. Nearly everyone raised their hand. " 'Kay, now, lousy food, lousy medical attention — how's that? We start with the services that were promised and not delivered."

He looked around, watching their faces. It was scoring. "The chair," he said calmly, deliberately, "would like to propose an inscription, for your approval, you know, suggest some language to the point of the preamble and —"

His eyes caught a couple in the corner of the crowded room making out. "Hey, come'n, that's out. This is serious." He rapped the cognac bottle. The offending couple parted quickly and looked around. Everyone gave them a hard stare. They were indulging themselves when they should be working on the *issue*.

"Take this down, Cora," Indian said quietly.

Everyone waited. He closed his eyes. "We, supporters of the North Atlantic Student Redress Assembly, do hereby declare —" He opened his eyes and looked around. They were hanging on every word. He stood, handed Ralph Rome the cognac bottle and moved as if to pace. The others made way for him. He took several steps and turned. He slouched. He wiped his face. He thought.

He looked around, "Okay so far? Listen, if anybody's got something to say, we're all communal here, speak up."

There was a chorus of approval.

"Stop me now, if anybody's got anything to say — *at all!* We don't want to go into this thing without knowing we all feel the same way and that we support everything in it, 'kay?"

There was another chorus of approval.

"Right," Indian said briskly. "Read that back to me, Cora, baby."

Cora cleared her throat. She was pleased with the way Indian was controlling the petition session. "We, supporters of the North Atlantic Students Redress Assembly, do hereby declare —" She paused and waited.

"Right," Indian said. ". . . that as free citizens, engaged in commercial transport of ourselves from one shore to another; lawfully engaged in a contract of trust and faith, whereby the Company, the Captain, the Officers and Crew have, through their acceptance of established rates of fare in *cash money,* acting as Agents for the Owners, denied promised contractual obligations. Failing, as Agents, to provide in the first case to passengers and students, now organized and known as the North Atlantic Students Redress Assembly (NASRA), signers and petitioners with contractual obligations entered into by the Passengers and the Owners, we give notice and demand redress."

Indian paused dramatically.

He looked around. They were galvanized. Cora was writing rapidly. She finished the last sentence, stopped and looked up at him.

"New paragraph. We address ourselves to Captain Abraham Coldwater, his Officers and Crew." Indian paused. "New paragraph. We address ourselves to, and appeal to those passengers in second and first class and invite them to join the North Atlantic Students Redress Assembly in its efforts to *secure* and *guarantee* rights and protection from the criminal behavior and acts of violence of Captain Abraham Coldwater, his Officers and Crew and, reestablish a cherished right of all citizens in voyage aboard any ship in the world, or any ocean, by name in all the world, *Freedom!*"

Indian had fallen into a hypnotic cadence. He watched them as he spoke. They were *listening*. He began to address the students in the cabin. G-703 became a rally: a meeting of the new religion. The faith was youth, the issue was freedom, the philosophy was *now,* the enemy was authority, the battleground was hypocrisy, the watchword was hang-ups, the ideal was eternal life, the discipline was anarchy, the belief was in a new thing, the dialogue was with any denying power, the militancy was against enforcing *their* demands, and the securing of ours.

"Freedom," Indian said in a low voice. "Freedoms. Freedoms! *Freedoms!*"

G-703 became a bedlam of approval. It roared its

134

approval with hugs and kisses and screams and shouts.

"Freedom! Freedom! Freedom! Now! Now! Now!"

Indian slumped. He waited. The shouts, the slaps on the shoulder, the kisses, meant nothing to him at all. He watched and waited for the right moment to turn it off.

" 'Kay, 'kay," he said, standing, holding up his hand. "So we're all together, so what? What does it mean? It means that we have to *stay* together, right?"

Another chorus of approval.

"Let's face it. We're going to be called excitement freaks. We're going to be called revolutionists. We're going to be called, in their stupid language, even maybe mutineers! But what are we going for?"

"Freedom!"

"Right," Indian said briskly. "Now let's get on with the redress items: anybody got any ideas?"

He slumped back. He had turned them on. The items came out in a tumble. Fuck the doctors! Fuck the food! Fuck the service! Fuck this — and fuck that . . .

"Great — *just great*," Indian said. "Listen, I've been in a few actions before, but you're lovely. You're sweet. You really know what it's all about; I love you. I love each and every one of you. You're what's going on, you're heavy people, man," Indian said. He squeezed out a tear. "You're what it's *all about*. I mean, it's easy, man, it's a *pleasure* to go out *front* for you —"

It started all over again. The girls kissed him. They grabbed for him. They tore at him. The boys pounded him on the back.

Cora watched it all. She knew what it was, but she couldn't resist. She started to cry. She and Ugly held each other and sobbed.

Indian found himself face to face with Rome. When he was sure no one was looking, he winked. "Let's get out of here," he whispered.

Ralph Rome hadn't really known until then what he was involved in and with whom. He nodded.

Indian stood up, his face shining wet. No one tried to stop him. He made his way quickly out of G-703; Rome made excuses about Indian being up tight and they would be back, and then followed him into the companionway.

They went to the tourist bar where the rock beat hammered at them. Indian bought a brandy. Then he turned on Rome. "Listen," he said coldly. "You were no fucking help in there *at all!* You know what I mean, man? Listen, we've *got* the bodies, cats who are turned on. Why didn't you get me out of there before I had to spitball that whole fucking redress preamble!"

136

Rome was stunned. He sat back in his chair. He couldn't find his voice. The coldness of Indian's sudden attack left him dumb.

"Well?" Indian demanded, this time less coldly.

"But I thought you wanted to do it. You were going so great!"

"Great my ass," Indian said. "It stinks. We'll write a very simple petition, using sixth grade English, without fancy language and phrases so that even the most ignorant members of the ship's crew can read and understand it. That whole thing back there was just to turn 'em on. We have a more serious problem —"

Indian sipped his brandy and brooded, his eyes sweeping the room. Rome was silent. He stared at his hands. Indian waved a few times or smiled and nodded as people passed their table, turning the charm on and then turning it off. "You want to be Number One, then get on the *ball!*"

Rome flared. "But how in the hell can you get them to believe in anything they don't participate in? They've got to believe it's them! The old shit about follow the leader is out. O-U-T! You're thinking like the rest of the shitheads, Che and Ho-Ho-Ho, and don't forget dear old stupid Fidel —"

"Dumb and stupid."

"All right, dumb and stupid. They're old hat, man.

Last year's scene." Rome began to take quick deep breaths to control his anger. "It's *all love and hate,* that's the bag, you saw them back there, sharing and sharing alike love and hate!"

"So?" Indian asked coolly. "What do you promise them?"

"You don't *promise* anything. You guarantee, baby. *Guarantee.*" Rome took another breath. "And another goddamn thing."

Indian had heard enough. He cut in quickly, flatly. "Now get on the ball, Rome. I don't want to be placed in the position of having to talk to those shitheads back in G-703 again, the way I did today."

"Yeah," Rome said heavily. "But you had to turn 'em on, didn't you? And you hadn't done *that* yet."

Indian looked at him quickly. Perhaps he was underestimating his Number One. "We have a problem."

"You mentioned it," Rome said with a careful dryness in his voice. "Well, speak, oh Chief."

"Get back in there and help them work out a draft of the petition. It shouldn't be too long. Not more than six or eight items, and stick to the facts, so I can fix it later. Dig?"

"Okay."

"And then go underground."

Rome sat up. "Underground?"

"Listen, as soon as good old Captain Coldwater gets a copy of this petition, he's going to come down here with the fucking Marines, right?"

"Right," Rome said, nodding. "Probably — yeah."

"And I think that the doctor is a smart ass. When it gets through his skull that there's action — organized action — he's going to tell it all and then they're going to come after me: *that's* why I say go underground. Move the whole Council every ninety minutes. I don't care where you go, cabins, into the john, gather in the open — *but move every ninety minutes,* you got me?"

"Sounds reasonable."

"And get hold of that big Alpaca, Nebraska, motorbike sapsucker. Enter a motion, get it passed and make him security head instead of the other little one with the big mouth. Take the big one to one side and talk 'em into the idea we need him. Pump him up. He's really a goony SS if I ever saw one, man, he's heavy."

Rome nodded. He was finding it difficult to keep up with Indian in his moves. But he appreciated them. He was almost in awe, accepting his dressing down with a grim determination to do better.

"Now, the action committees." Indian finished his brandy and signaled for another. "We've got to get several typewriters — and typists. Probably some of the square, up-tight chicks aboard have them. Find out and recruit them. The most difficult is going to be to get stencil papers for mimeos and a mimeo machine. Before the war starts."

"The *war!*"

Indian nodded casually. "War as pure as Gettysburg — Iwo Jima — the Battle of the Bulge. But never mind that now. Find out about the mimeo machine —"

"That ought to be pretty easy."

"I should think so," Indian said casually, "for a Number One."

"Ah, come'n, Indian. Don't lean so hard."

"Back to the action committees. That cat with the camera. I want him around me at all times. I want the whole thing recorded, got it?"

"Okay. He'll flip out. He's *already* flipped out, over the idea of getting real live action."

"And I want him to frame it in such a way that we can lip sync it later — you know? Over-record in case we have to."

"Got it. I'll challenge him," Rome said.

"Now, you're acting like Number One," Indian said with a smile. "Take that Fat Cat and supervise his work-up of precedence and practice. See if he knows anything about the Puritans, you know, when they split from England and went to Holland and if there was any trouble on the boats going over to the States —"

"Check."

"Don't you think you had better take notes?" Indian asked.

"And have it fall into enemy hands?" Rome asked deadpan.

"Okay, Number One, any way you want to do it. Now — for Ugly — she's very important. We want to get a foreign flavor to this — international abstracts are always very good. See if you can't get her to do some speechmaking since she knows so goddamn many languages —"

"How about getting her and Fat Cat Middle English Politics together and giving them a thing to do?"

"*That's what I mean*, Number One!" Indian said. "Now you're timing it perfectly. You're coming in four-oh, baby. Four-oh."

"Right! What else?"

"Big Mouth," Indian said. "She's very important. She's got the gossipy thing going for her, you know? I mean with the signs of the zodiac and all that shit, right?"

"Right."

"Tell her to work up a horoscope; give it the right sign, like Venus is in Mars's house and —"

"Getting laid," Rome said with a smile.

141

"That's it, Number One, that's it."

"What's this coming over?" Rome nodded across the dance floor.

Indian looked up. It was the girl with her own cabin. She swayed up to the table. "Hello, Stud." She touched Indian's cheek.

"No time, sweetie, no time."

"Definitely passive," the girl said. She smoothed her hair and looked at Rome.

"Only for aggressive chicks like you," Indian said. "Why don't you tune into something else besides your crotch?"

"Truth and beauty maybe?" the girl said. "Like, whose truth? And what beauty?"

"I'm talking about political action. And you're still hung up on infantile sex."

"Oh Christ, a Marxist freak!" She turned away without looking at him again.

"One more thing," Indian said to Rome as they both watched the girl walk away and continue her prowl. "Ling Jung. Very important."

"In what way?"

"Groove him into deadpan attrition. I want a stalemate. I want a Paris peace talker with an ass hard enough to sit there."

"Why?" Rome looked at him puzzled.

"Coldwater can take us out in two ways. He can grant all the demands, and in three days it's all over. We're in New York and he's rid of us."

"That would be pretty smart of him," Rome conceded.

"*And* he can grab us *all* off in the Action Council and send in the salt-water hose crews again." Indian lit a cigarette. "I want him to grab *me*. And *only* me. That's why you go underground and keep it cool, and then start the hunger strikes and the sit-ins *in first and second class* to get *me* out of the can —"

"Jesus!" Rome said, genuinely impressed. "Got it! Got it all."

Indian stood suddenly.

"Where are you going?"

"Meet you in a half-hour. Either here, or back in 703. Watch it, here come two masters-at-arms. Take a good look at them and point them out to our security."

Indian walked away and at the door of the companionway he turned back and watched as Rome sized up the two ship's security officers. They wore buffalo pants, leather vests and flower shirts, and love beads flopped on their chests. They were about as easy in their costumes as a Notre Dame School Sister might be with a Sten gun.

Indian separated himself from the Action Council and their commune of love-hate and the process of hammering out the Petition of Redress, and wandered around the ship. There was no way that he could see that he could miss. He had, so far, made a perfect pyramid. All he needed now was one more incident to bring him to the attention of Coldwater, then he was sure he would be arrested.

He leaned on the boat-deck railing and listened to the laughter and conversations of those who strolled the decks, enjoying their voyage, and wondered suddenly what it would be like to be an old person.

Not aged or infirm, but older, twenty years older — forty-four or -five. What would his life have brought him? One thing he was sure of, he was going into politics. Real power — money power and military power — was *there*. It was just a question of application of what he had learned about power. So far he had been flexing the muscles of his mind, expanding them, and it, to take in the whole world.

He was amazed to discover how easy it was to get up a game of follow the leader.

'Kay, he thought, they would do *anything*. But how to use it, apply it. First though, he would have to get inside the present power structures and observe the rules and then look for their weaknesses; then he was

144

sure that he would work outside the present establishment.

A beautiful young girl laughed. Her happiness floated up and out over the railing into the ocean air like sun after a summer shower. He turned and looked at her. Marriage, certainly, Indian thought, and to a rich one who would share his interests and could supply the heavy money he would need.

Where did he want to go? He wanted to go as far as life would take him, he thought. How much did he want? He wanted it all — no, he corrected, staring out over the water, he wanted *more*.

He stepped up on the bottom rung of the railing, braced his knees on the second rung and held out his arms and hands, making a V over his head, his fingers outstretched. World, he thought, smiling, feeling the richness of his dreams shower down on him, it's just you and me. As much as you are, that's what I'm going to have.

The strollers and the sunbathers observed the young man with the Indian-style headband, and who looked so much like a real Indian, and watched his antics and smiled. Youth, it was wonderful.

The executive members of the Action Council completed the Petition of Redress with nine items under the close supervision of Rome, and then, with each of them fully instructed in their assignments, left G-703 after having set a rendezvous for an hour and a half later in the tourist library to check each other's progress. A mimeo machine had been located in the second-class pantry, one used for sending out general notices to the crew, and Rome made this his own personal assignment. He took several of the bike security people and staged a mock fight to create a diversion while he grabbed the machine. Ugly, with her fluency in five languages rippling off her tongue, began to circulate and drop hints about the Action Council. She was a remarkable success: she met resistance in only one group of students, those who had managed to slip out of Czechoslovakia during the invasion, who scornfully derided her attempts at recruiting them. Ugly had nothing to say when they accused her of being immature and not appreciating the basic freedoms of the West. Big Mouth picked up a small but fervent fringe group among the Signs followers. Fat Cat and Ling Jung worked together on precedence and it was all very carefully recorded by the Film Maker. An hour and a half later they slipped into the library one at a time and held a briefing session. They had made, it was agreed, re-markable headway. The little-used tourist gym would be their next rendezvous ninety minutes later. They

146

were building Indian's pyramid, one that could not miss.

Indian may or may not have built a perfect pyramid, but he was not a stupid young man and he knew there were sixteen hundred students in the ship among whom were freaks of many different natures. He continued to wander the ship, sniffing, searching, looking for openings and advantages he might be able to put to use. He mentally listed the splinter groups, freakies, which by definition meant anyone who was not square. There were sex freaks, theater-film-art freaks, freaks who made the drug scene, freaks who were straight-establishment political activists, militancy freaks who sought out minorities to support, and then the wide gulf separating these from the vast majority of students who were, simply, square.

In the first thirty-six hours of the voyage, Indian had observed many isolated fights among the students. Most of these started with an invasion by one or the other of the freakies into the square world of the very-nice-and-good. It was rarely the other way around, he noted.

The square world was the one area he was not sure of, and in which he could not predict a reaction.

The structured world of the *establishment* was his
meat; decayed and crumbly at the core and therefore
easy to puncture and destroy. But he worried about
the sincere world of the squares. He had seen the
fragmented freakies join together many times and
forge a solid front against the squares and he knew
that this was a result of the separation which was as
clean as right and left between the two main bodies
of students. If you were a freakie, no matter what
your scene was, then you were not a square. If you
wanted to return home and go to college, or to
General Motors or Wall Street, or if you did not
question American involvement in Vietnam, then you
were a square. If you had Other interests, then you
were a freakie.

Indian compared the two groups to the separation
that followed the Reformation. Either you were a
Catholic, or you were not. It did not matter what the
divisions were among the Protestants, they were *all*
against the Vatican.

He dropped to the lower deck, borrowed a pair of
trunks and took a salt-water swim in the truncated
pool. He swung on the ropes and listened and
watched the activities around him.

His main worry about the world of the square
students had been for a long time their obviousness.

They had objectives and a healthy smattering of identity. They seemed to have accepted their role as emotionally immature adults, growing up in a harsh pragmatic world and, adjusting to the demands made on them, gradually emerging at the other end of their young lives quite capable of making tough decisions. The freakies, by contrast, moved from presence to presence, forcing themselves into finding a fix as each identity crisis arose, then reacting with compulsive behavior to prove to themselves they were not of the square world.

He dressed slowly and had a cup of tea and sat near a huge picture window and studied the shifting, ever changing sea.

In many ways, he himself identified with the square world. They had objectives, and so did he, while the freakies had none. He had never really been able to understand the infantile, kindergarten compulsions of the freak scenes. They reminded him of a frustrated child drawing on the walls with a crayon, or biting another child in anger over a disagreement, or banging its head. To him, as he listened to the talk flowing around him, some serious, some concerned, some gay, some hysterical, the freakies were monsters. Not only were they childish, but scared and naïve. But, he sighed to himself, if

149

that was their bag, then it was only sensible to take advantage of their psyched compulsions.

He wandered back up to the boat deck.

A subsidized revolution was under way in most of the Western world, profound and distinct in character from any other in history that he was aware of. The sincere objectives of the square fathers and mothers who supported the freakies and their pursuit of identity were so close to Indian's own objectives, that at times in the past he had almost felt ashamed of taking advantage of them.

But he was not, this time, concerned with the freakies. He had lived with them and their compulsions too long and had examined their immaturity too closely to be anything but contemptuous of their behavior. It was the solid, formidable mass of the new generation's establishment-supporting squares that concerned him most.

He smiled to himself. Taking off his headband, he let the wind blow his hair dry. It had always amazed him that in articles and books on the New Generation the authors consistently missed the point by lumping everyone under twenty-five into the same bag. In fact there was more of a communication gap between the freakies and the squares than there was between one generation and the next. And in many ways, Indian concluded, the differences were greater

and as genuinely demonstrable. The problem of turning on the squares had been, from the start, the most
difficult one for him to solve.

And then the problem was solved and the solution
fell into his hands.

The squares advertised an action happening
among the students, and that afternoon, first and
second class went slumming to the tourist bar where,
it was rumored in an exciting whisper, the students
were putting on a little theatrical and they were
going to take their clothes off.

But it wasn't the squares who staged the happening who took off their clothes, It was an invasion of
sex freakies who had been very carefully rounded up
by Indian, Cora and Rome. And that started the kind
of chain reaction that was made in heaven for the
North Atlantic Students Redress Assembly. Indian
could move in on the scene with his already functioning Action Council cadre with the ease of a commanding general, which in the purest sense he was.

The rumor was accurate. It *was* a happening. It
started out as a predictable pretense of living-drama
theater. The script was the brainchild of Winston
Beauchamp, a stylish young man who wrote terribly
intense plays about the plight of the Blacks, the
mountain Whites of West Virginia heavily larded

with power words and phrases: "We gunna have ta git Whitey, man, yo heah!" and "It don't seem right a man wuk hissef to a hole in the ground and don't ever see the sun." Winston Beauchamp wore a mandarin beard and Edwardian jackets and spoke with a Harvard accent. He was sensitive, by his own declaration, and up tight about the world situation which he thought could be explained through a living theater. The happening which he wrote and directed was on such a theme.

The cast and crew were assembled, all as eager as puppies to get involved with life and the theater. It had not been hard for Winston Beauchamp to recruit his fellows of the theater. The salon lights were dimmed, darkened, then went to black. The crew stood by nervously, telling each other good luck and break a leg.

Several boys and girls — all beautiful — entered the darkened tourist bar-salon wearing bikinis, and proceeded to repeat, variously, three phrases. They wore Genêt masks (to suggest their need for anonymity and their yearning to free themselves of guilt) and everyone was very solemn and intent and thrilled and full of good raunchy anticipation.

Mary Coffin, a pert little redhead with a beautiful body, was the first on stage. A spotlight hit her. "Love me and Love Other!" she cried in a screeching voice, her arms extended in a gesture of hope, then she did a kindergarten ballet step and skipped offstage.

"Take it —" a voice shouted, but the light was in the wrong place, and there was a dizzying moment as the light sought out the body behind the voice. "Take it and shove it!" a nearly nude Joe Kazzipi bawled, then dropped his hands and arms and head and stood still.

The light hit a much older woman, she looked to be at least thirty. She wore a stocking foundation and nothing underneath. When the light hit her, everything was revealed. She took a few motherly steps toward Joe Kazzipi, turned and faced the audience. "Mother and Father and Jesus are sacred words!" she cried.

"Show us your tits, baby!" somebody shouted from the audience.

The cast ignored the remark. Then Mary Coffin returned on stage, and joined in a carefully rehearsed but poorly timed group scene; the cadence faltered, spluttered.

"Love me —"

"Father —"

"Shove it, Mother —"

"Take it, Jesus —"

While this was going on, several other characters (who represented Father, Love Other and Jesus) slipped into the darkened room. They all carried pots of water paint and brushes and proceeded to paint the nearly nude bodies of the actors and each other with Nazi swastikas, the Star of David, KKK, the Cross of Calvary.

"These are the signs of hate — and love!" Mary Coffin said to the audience. "We must learn to love each other — Love Other!"

"Never mind that crap — take off your clothes!" someone in the audience shouted.

There was a roar of approval from the crowd in the darkened bar.

The audience began to participate, and while a running projector flashed old Laurel and Hardy films on the walls and the ceiling, the loudspeakers were suddenly turned on full volume and "Little Green Apples," at half the normal beat, filled the room with sugary sentiment.

Indian had stood in the doorway of the bar with his bike security and a half-dozen girls. He turned and nodded. "Now," he said quietly. They began to push through the crowd to the dance floor.

Now the painters were rushing into the audience to paint the noses and faces and ears of the onlookers; they splashed paint on anyone and everyone. The volume was turned up full on the amplifier. The audience began to get up and dash onto the dance floor that served as a stage. Indian's girls reached the dance floor. They began to strip. Shocked, Winston Beauchamp rushed out and tried to drag them off the floor. The audience roared at him to leave them alone. The girls pulled away, and laughing hysterically, continued to take off their clothes, ripping off their bras and panties. The audience clapped and roared its approval. The actors turned their paint-brushes on the new nudies and daubed them from head to toe with color. The first- and second-class passengers, like the audience at a cockfight, stood on their chairs and cheered and urged the students on.

Not everyone, however, was turned on. Several couples tried to leave, but they were turned back at the doors of the bar by Indian's bike security, acting under his direction, who insisted they stay with the happening.

That was when the fights broke out and the whole scene turned into a screaming, yelling, fighting, vicious mob. "Little Green Apples" continued to play over the riot. The lights were turned out. The young man handling the projector was knocked over and sparks flashed when the electric connections were disrupted. Dressed, half-dressed and totally nude bodies turned the action happening into a nightmare of seething movement and bodily violence. And still the bike security at the door would not let anyone out. They kept the doors closed, slamming their bodies against the doors and holding the line.

The first- and second-class passengers, caught in this madness, panicked. They came at the bike security with chairs and tried to force the doors open. The students retaliated. The younger, stronger bodies tore into the soft middle-aged ones like hot knives going through butter.

Lulu Tennington, who had attended with her photographer husband, was knocked cold. Her husband was bloodied when he tried to protect her. Sir Harry Weldon, who had only stood at the edge of the salon near the doors, backed up against the bulkhead and held his hands out before him in a pathetic attempt to ward off the missiles that were hurtling through the air; he was finally thrown to the deck, where he lay moaning and writhing in pain.

Once again sailors came with hoses. They were grim and experienced. They aimed ice-cold seawater under seventy pounds of pressure into the bike security holding the doors and sprayed them around like rag dolls. Another group of sailors led by the masters-at-arms moved in with rubber truncheons and rapped everything they saw, arms, legs, knees, wrists, necks, heads. They opened the doors.

"Oh my good God in heaven," Coldwater breathed. The tourist salon was nothing like anything he had ever seen before. He flashed his light around. Arms, legs, blood, bodies, the moans and cries of the wounded, the bloody faces, the totality of the destruction was overwhelming.

Dr. Jaca and the entire hospital staff had rushed to the salon. There Jaca stopped. He stood just inside the doorway a moment. A young boy stared up at him, his mouth a mass of blood. Jaca started to tremble with rage.

"Groovy, eh, Doc?" Indian said at his side.

"*You!*" Jaca said hoarsely. "I knew — I *knew* —"

"Now hold on, Doc — cool it, man — I wasn't even here."

"This is the man responsible, Captain," Jaca said, barely able to restrain himself from grabbing Indian.

"Arrest him," Coldwater said harshly. Two masters-at-arms grabbed the unresisting, pliant Indian and hustled him away.

6

You Know What They Call It— The Age of Aquarius...

IN THE TOURIST BAR, the students struck back at the sailors with cold fury. This was not an organized, planned, coordinated attack led by Indian up on the skyline waving a banner, nor was it a mob prepped by Ralph Rome into an assault, nor did it degenerate into horseplay like the earlier breakfast incident; this was a total gut reaction by all of the students to the hosing, the rubber truncheons, the hard-line suppression of their physical freedoms. And of course no one stopped to figure out that it was a group of students themselves who had held the doors closed, which precipitated the panic.

Bar stools were ripped from their fastenings and used as clubs. Chairs were thrown thirty feet into the hard knot of sailors, who fought back with hoses and clubs. The cries, the screams, the curses, the oaths in a half-dozen languages were of one voice. Coldwater was struck on the shoulder with a chair and thrown to the deck. Chief Officer Reggie was caught by six students and beaten unmercifully in retaliation for four sailors cornering a long-haired student and working him over with a sureness that would have done Chicago cops proud. Jaca was thrown to the deck and his medical bag kicked to one side, its contents spilled out over the deck, delicate syringes and instruments crushed in the mass of feet.

More sailors and ship's crew were brought in for reinforcements. The tide began to turn when the students were hemmed in from both sides and gradually the crew whittled their way through the surging mob. After fifteen minutes of this, it was over. Thirty-one students were arrested and confined. But not one member of the North Atlantic Students Redress Assembly was involved.

The moment Indian had been arrested, Ralph Rome had slipped away with the executive member of the Action Council and had gone underground. By the time the crew had firm control of the students and the tourist decks were secure, the Action Council had cut stencils and were grinding out copies of the Redress Petition — which Indian had almost casually rewritten on the back of a menu card while having coffee. By the time order had been restored and Jaca was once more bandaging cuts and bruises and the scattering of first-class passengers had fled to the sanctuary of the upper decks, ninety copies a minute of the petition were being struck off the mimeo machine and distributed throughout the ship.

THE NORTH ATLANTIC STUDENTS REDRESS ASSEMBLY

DEMANDS

1. Amnesty for all passengers arrested.
2. Charges be brought against Captain Abraham Coldwater for criminal acts of violence.
3. Immediate dismissal of Dr. Luis Jaca for incompetence.
4. Charges be brought against Chief Steward Bolton for serving rotten food and for graft.
5. Freedom of the ship for all passengers in all classes.

This is not a mutiny. No attempt will be made to take over the direction, or the propulsion of the ship, or assume the authority that lawfully and rightfully belongs to the ship's officers. It is a Petition of Redress for the flagrant breach of contract by the Company, Captain Coldwater, the Officers and Crew, and a denial of basic freedoms.

THESE DEMANDS ARE NOT NEGOTIABLE

Action Council
NASRA

Within an hour after the petition was circulated, the coalition of the left and the right, the freakies and the squares, so necessary to Indian's plans, was achieved. Ralph Rome moved in on the confusion, and with members of the Action Council marshaling support and browbeating the opposition, he assumed leadership in Indian's name. There was one bad moment when Winston Beauchamp tried to assume leadership, but Rome, with Cora's help, put him down. The first order of business was put forth. Riding the crest of the emotional wave, Rome presented his first demands to the body of students and received a roaring, overwhelming approval.

"We *sit* in! We *hit* back! We go on *hunger* strikes! We do not move. We *resist* — until — until — *listen to me!*" He could hardly complete his sentence, his thought, his idea. They did not care. They wanted revenge. "We do *nothing* until *Indian* and all the others are released from prison!"

Over one thousand students agreed. Several hundred did not. The leather-jacketed bike group moved in and protected Ralph Rome as if he were President of the United States, fending off any and all objectors, playing their role of security with the same cruel and indifferent thoroughness as all security men the world over. The crew members stationed around the restless moving mob of students watched and listened and did not understand at all.

The brig aboard the S.S. *New York* in which Indian was placed, separated from the others, was a simple steel vault with a bed, basin and toilet. Indian accepted his prison with a detachment and calmness that was misunderstood by the chief master-at-arms as the well-known second thoughts, or what-in-the-hell-have-I-done-now attitude. The chief master-at-arms had seen it many times. He peeked through the opening of the half-inch steel-plate door and grunted with the somber satisfaction of a man who has been proven right again. They were always sorry when he closed the door behind them. He retired to his desk and continued to read a sensational novel about a spy named Monty Nash who, he was convinced, was the baddest sonofabitch alive and fortunately on our side. The ship's roll and vibration eased him back into his fantasy as easily as a mother hushabying an infant. Inside the vault, Indian settled himself and started doing Yoga exercises, completely relaxed, and for the moment suspended in time.

The shock vibrations of the riot that had stemmed from the pathetic attempt at a theatrical happening swept through the great vessel, first, second, tourist and crew, like a giant wave that had sprung up out of a fault in the ocean floor. By evening, everyone aboard had seen the petition. That night, dinner was quiet. Cocktail parties were either canceled or very, very hushed and subdued. Couples who had started romantic involvements were robbed of the illusion that they were for a moment indulging in a simple reality that would last for a few days and then disappear when the ship arrived in New York. They would never forget it as long as they lived.

The French Room was nearly deserted at the cocktail hour. The band played with forced enthusiasm and idle waiters and stewards and busboys watched the doors nervously as if expecting an invasion at any moment. In second class, passengers wandered around in a state of total disbelief; they shook their heads often and with looks of despair.

And in tourist the war was continuing, but on a different level. It was openly hostile staring contests between the students and the waiters and stewards; cold, silent and tense. The crew, however, was different. It was the generally accepted opinion in the crew mess that night, with many conversations rolling and rerolling over each other, that Captain Coldwater was going to slam down hard. They could not imagine there was any force on the face of the earth that could make Captain Coldwater, master of the finest ship in the world, with international law and authority on his side, backed by three thousand years of historical precedents and the traditionally absolute imperiousness of the sea, bow to the demands of the Redress Petition.

The ship was alive with rumors. Gossip ebbed and

flowed with the sureness of a tide, generating distracting currents and whirlpools of intense speculation on what was going to happen, be done — and how.

Only a very few in first class went into the French Room for the cabaret entertainment and dancing that night. Even fewer in second class went to see Burt Lancaster in *Six-Gun Vengeance*. And because of the curfew set down by Coldwater on the tourist section, the students ate their roast beef and hash browns and slipped quietly and inconspicuously from one room to another.

Only the crew section was anything near normal. They played bridge and checkers; and with the second-class theaters nearly empty, some of them dressed in their best clothes and slipped topside and enjoyed the movie.

And everyone waited to see what Captain Coldwater was going to do about the petition. Everyone, that is, except Jaca.

"No, Eustace," Coldwater said tiredly to the designer-builder of the S.S. *New York*. "No, it's not too badly damaged. They just tore out a few bar stools and wall fixtures and busted a few chairs. Nothing insurance won't cover and it won't bother our turnaround in New York. I've already talked to Eric

167

Kaufmann in New York. They're all alert for the fitters to come aboard —" Stern massaged Coldwater's shoulder where he had been struck with the chair. "You betcha sweet ass I'm going to keep them in the brig!" Coldwater shouted into the phone. "There isn't anything on this ocean that can keep me from doing it either. Well, hell, Eustace, I can't do that. No, I'm not going to press charges — no, no, now listen to me, Eustace, they're nothing but kids. I can't go in there and slap 'em around as if they were deck sailors in a mutiny! Yes, dammit, yes!" Coldwater began to lose patience with the designer-builder of the finest ship afloat. "I notified the Coast Guard — both sides — England and ours. But I'm at the point of no return — just as easy to go forward as it is to go back, and how would it look to the public if I had to turn around? — yes, exactly thirty-five west at four bells this evening. No, the low pressure didn't develop. I wish to Christ it would. I'd love to have, for the first time in my life as a sailor, a big, whole gale. I'd open the bar and let 'em all get drunk and seasick and that would be the end of it, but it's like a sheet of glass out here tonight. Listen, Eustace, I'm tired and I've got a problem on my hands, and there isn't a hell of a lot you can do to help me. So, I'm going to hang up now and try to get a little rest."

Coldwater hung up the phone. He immediately

picked up a thick stack of reports each department head had made on the damage that had been done during the riots and began to sift through them.

"Captain?" Stern worked on the shoulder.

Captain Coldwater did not look up. "Yeah."

"Dr. Jaca is here."

Coldwater looked up at Jaca who had appeared in the captain's suite without knocking. "Hello, Luis, anything wrong?"

Jaca held a copy of the petition in his hand. "I'd like to talk to you, Captain."

"Go ahead."

"Alone."

Without a word, or a moment's hesitation, Stern slipped toward the door. Jaca stopped him. "I want a double bourbon and water, please."

Jaca sat down and wiped his face. He had deep circles under his eyes. His face was haggard. He wore a slight, startlingly white gauze bandage on his wrist where he had been cut with a piece of glass. Neither man spoke until Jaca had his drink. "I'd like a half-hour, Stern. Alone with the captain. If you can manage that?"

Stern looked at Coldwater, who nodded. The door closed.

"Abe," Jaca said easily, and then looked up quickly, a faint smile on his face, "I'm not calling you

169

Captain, because this is an unofficial visit, and because right now you're a very vulnerable man and you need help, the help of a friend, and I'd like to think of myself as your friend."

"I understand," Coldwater said. "Say what you have to say."

"I want to tell you something — a story — a true story — because I want you to know my credentials. You're a good man, Abe, so — well, I've never told anyone — but you must know to understand why I'm here —"

Coldwater nodded and waited.

He started to talk. The energy surged through him like electricity. He paced the deck. Captain Coldwater sat and watched him, at times feeling Jaca's terror, at other times feeling his own.

". . . my sister was small, too delicate for the heavy work of a nurse in a small town like Tunas de Zaza; but, well, Maria and I had a childhood dream, we used to talk during our siesta, how I would be the doctor and she would be the nurse and we would have our own hospital. Well, I went to the States, Harvard, and she went into training in Havana —

". . . Fidel and Che had already landed and were raiding all over the island. One night the government troops came to Tunas de Zaza. They had been

warned there would be a raid. They were waiting. It
was a trap. They hunted the rebels down like dogs
and killed them all — the wounded — everybody —
taking no prisoners. Three rebels had fled to the hospital and were hidden in the basement. My sister was
taking care of them. The troops came in and opened
fire. They killed everyone, including my sister. Then
they came for me in Havana. I was in prison for four
months . . .

"They would not believe that I knew nothing about
the Tunas de Zaza raid or that my sister was not one
of the rebels. They tortured me and when I had
nothing to confess, they brought a young girl in and
gang-raped her. Before they were through, fourteen
men had attacked her. She didn't utter a sound.
Then, they simply shot her in the head. A few days
after that, they let me go, I'll never know why, and
I went back to our house in Matanzas. It was about
then that I was sent word that Che wanted to see
me. We arranged a meeting. He wanted me, he said,
to join them in the hills. They needed doctors. Fidel
had sent him personally. It soon came out that they
were just trying to exploit my hatred for Batista, and
my grief over Maria, for their own purposes. I was
nearly taken in. But by then I had heard pretty re-
liable stories about *their* treatment of government
troops. It was the same on both sides, and of course

171

the world found out all about it later when they had their revolutionary trials in the sports arena like a Roman circus . . .

"Anyway, I refused. So Che promised me that I would be in charge of all the hospitals and medical services when they took over; it was to be the first priority after food. I still refused. I was sick of it. Four months of torture and starvation, the brutality in the prison, that poor girl raped and executed; all of it had turned me away from life itself and shriveled me up on the inside like a dried fig. There was nothing left. When I finally convinced Che that I was not going to join them in Oriente, he warned me not to remain in Cuba after they had taken over. I took the warning seriously. I left soon after that . . .

"So. Then came the Miami period. In many ways that was the worst. Washing dishes in Miami Beach hotels, watching the gringos indulge themselves to the point of nausea, stuffing themselves at night, then having the fat massaged off during the day. I tried getting a job in a hospital as an orderly, but I couldn't stand the sight of anything that was frail or delicate, or needed help. Moans of pain from the patients brought it all back to me. I fled. Back to the hotels and washing dishes. Then my feeling shifted the other way, the opposite extreme. I was enraged again. Exiles were drifting into Miami by then. Hun-

dreds of them, fleeing *both* Batista and Fidel. I joined
a group who did nothing but arrange to take people
out of Cuba. It did not make any difference who they
were, or what they had done, or from which side
they were fleeing. It made no difference. It created
problems of course. Once in a while a rebel who had
fallen out of favor with Fidel would spot a Batista
official and there would be a fight, sometimes a
murder; but it did not affect me at all. I was working
out my rage against both of them, with no motive
other than to serve those who were in jeopardy. Then
that period, too, finally ended . . .

"It was a dark night, and it was so quiet you could
hear your heart beat. I ran a boat out of Saturday
Key near Marathon, over to Matanzas. All we did,
two men and a boy, was pick up those who wanted to
get out. That night there was no moon. We had tried
four times to get in close, but they had developed a
technique where they used Jeeps with machine guns
mounted on the back and patrolled the coasts and
beaches looking for raiders. Two men and a boy. An
old Communist that had been thrown out by Che for
being a revisionist and a boy who had heard nothing
but the honor of this, and the honor of that, and that
is *his* honor, and this is *my* honor, and that is *their*
honor, all of his life. And he was with us that night
because he had been shamed into it. Well, we got

into the quiet water. It was nearly perfect, but we were afraid of the machine-gun-mounted Jeeps. Fear. It was worse in some ways than what I had known in the Havana prison. I vomited. The boy, who was only seventeen, wet his pants, but he hung in there. The old one had to remove his false teeth so he could breathe, in and out, in and out through his loose lips . . .

"But he hung in there, too. We slid into the beach; then the people came out of the vegetation like lost souls, or ghosts, struggling down to the rafts the boy and the old man had paddled ashore. Then the lights struck. They opened fire. They murdered everyone — they killed them all — and I ran forward and grabbed a life jacket and lowered myself into the water and started swimming out into the gulf. I prayed the sharks would come. I didn't want to live anymore. The world had gone mad. It was insane. The luxury at Miami Beach — the murder, rape, cruelty in Cuba by both sides — but I could not put my head underwater and drown. Something kept me from doing it; I tried, but I could never quite do it.

". . . From there to New York and living in a room in Harlem. I washed dishes again. And once I sold newspapers at a Times Square kiosk. I drifted. I didn't think: I turned it off. And then little by little I began to get back my sense of being and who I was. I

174

tried to work in a hospital again as an orderly, and gradually I overcame the past, like a man who has been a drug addict most of his life and finally finds the spark of strength he needs to kick it. . . ."

They sat silently. Jaca had not touched his drink. It sat, watery now from the melting ice. They both smoked and listened to the murmur of the ship as it drove through the sea.

"Why do you tell me this now — what has brought it on?" Coldwater asked.

"Why now?" Jaca asked in reply. "Because now there is another one aboard this ship. Down there in the tourist section. Another Che — another Fidel — another Ho — another Hitler, perhaps. I know every move he's making. Not necessarily Communist but a destroyer."

Coldwater looked at him. "You mean the students."

Jaca nodded. "I thought it was over, all over. My hatred for violence and thoughtless, witless cruelties. I thought I could doctor the sick and wounded and infirm and hide. And I have hidden. That's why I came aboard this ship. I didn't want anything permanent, anything that could force me to look, ever to look again. I thought it was over for me in other areas as well. The dialogue, for instance. *Why are they doing it?* What's wrong with the world? I never thought I'd ask that question again, or care."

"Luis — "

"I never thought I would be *engaged* again. I don't even know *how* I am engaged." He closed his eyes. "All I am sure of at the moment is that the hate is rising again. Like a wound being ripped open —"

. The phone rang. "Yes, he's here." Coldwater handed him the receiver.

"Yes. Yes, yes, I understand." He hung up the phone. "That was my nurse. The Peterson girl just died. She never regained — she never knew anything — I mean —"

He moved toward the door.

"Luis —" Coldwater commanded. "Sit down. If she's dead, there's nothing you can do. Sit down."

"Do you know," Jaca said quietly, "what's actually happening aboard the ship?"

"What do you mean?"

"Do you understand what's at the bottom of this?"

"They've spelled out a lot of garbage in their petition. Which isn't worth used toilet paper."

"You're wrong, Abe," Jaca said slowly. "Very wrong. You're about to lose your ship."

"What!"

"And your career, and perhaps even be disgraced."

Abraham Coldwater turned white. His lips compressed. "Nothing, and no-goddamn-body is going to hurt me or this ship, my passengers or crew."

"Abe — Abe," Jaca said softly and very quietly, "listen to me a minute." He sat forward in his chair, holding his drink, his head hanging a little. He stared at the carpeting. He was tired. As tired as he had ever been in his life. "You're up against something you know absolutely nothing about. Nothing."

"Don't be so sure," Coldwater said. "One appeal on the five hundred frequency and I could have half of the Navy from the States and France and England here in —"

"I know it, Abe. You know it. What's more important, *they* know it."

"Who the hell is — are — *they!*"

Jaca sipped his drink and held up the petition. "The North Atlantic Students Redress Assembly. You're the focal point in a conspiracy. They mean to rip this ship apart. *Not* take it over, just destroy it — and you — and me. And anything else that gets in the way."

"Can you prove that?" Coldwater stood and hovered over Jaca.

"Listen to me, first, just listen."

"Can you *prove* it? Have you got evidence?"

"No, I can't," Jaca said patiently. "But, if you'll listen, I can make a damn good case for the grand jury — *you*, in this case, being the grand jury. You want to listen, or let it go?"

"Go ahead," Coldwater said. He sat down. "Go on."

"Do you think your behavior has been criminal?"

"Not at all."

"Do you think that I'm incompetent?"

"You know the answer to that."

"How about Chief Steward Bolton — do you think, knowing him as you do, do you think he would serve food to anyone that he suspected for a moment might not be the finest, freshest and prepared as well as it can be done?

"Or do you think he would *steal* anything? Graft?"

Coldwater did not reply. He just shook his head.

"Then why?"

"Why what?"

"Why has this petition been mimeographed and spread around the ship? Did you know that the machine was stolen yesterday?"

"No."

"Did you know that this petition was flooding the ship within an hour after the riot?"

"No."

"It's a conspiracy, Abe."

"But they don't *want* to take over the ship."

"And that is a point well taken. *This is not a mutiny,*" Jaca read from the petition. "*No attempt will be made to take over the direction, or the propulsion of the ship, or assume the authority that lawfully and rightfully belongs to the ship's officers.*" Jaca threw the paper to one side. "What is their motive?"

"I don't know." Coldwater said, settling back and listening.

"I do," Jaca said. "When is the last time you went ashore?"

"Why?"

"Tell me."

"Couple of trips ago, in New York."

"Ever read the papers?"

"Sure —"

"*Time, Life, Newsweek?*"

"Every week."

"Ever watch television?"

"How can I?"

"Never seen the student riots on television? What happened in Chicago?"

"No. Is it important?"

"I'm asking you," Jaca said.

"I don't think, if you come right down to it, that it's important."

"And that, Abe, is why I'm here. To tell you how

important it is and — they are — and what's going on. You've isolated yourself in a narrow, restricted world of the sea and ships. You're at the top of the heap. And you deserve it. But you don't know what's going on out there — not just in the States, but throughout the whole world."

Slow realization of what Jaca was saying to him settled over Coldwater. His face filled with color. "You mean — they have no reason at all for doing what they're doing?"

"None," Jaca said, "Oh, there are legitimate issues expressed by militant minorities — but that's small, diffuse, and by and large, honest political action. But elsewhere? What about them?"

"Where elsewhere?" Coldwater asked.

"The May–June riots in France? What about them?"

Captain Abraham Coldwater stood again. He began to pace the deck. He did not look at Jaca. Automatically, as he did a dozen times a day, he picked up the phone and spoke to the bridge. "Where are we?" He listened. "All right — keep a sharp lookout." He hung up the phone and paced some more. "Go ahead, Luis."

"France — nineteen sixty-eight. Two months of absolute chaos. I've heard the figure was six billion dollars lost — people were seriously injured — killed — and a government nearly fell. An important part of civilization, almost, as they say, wasted. And with it, cutbacks in government grants, loans, farm subsidies to the chicken farmers in rural France who are now in desperate need, factory workers deeper in debt. And so on — what for, Abe? What for? What was their motive? They are not Communists like Castro, they are not fascists like those in South Africa — what are they? They're destroyers. With contempt for only one thing. Discipline."

"I don't believe that, Luis — I can't."

"Remember Colonel Peterson yesterday?"

"But — but —"

"Multiply that by millions. In every country in the world. And they aren't out to make a better world, regardless of what they say. They're not. *That* doesn't make them dangerous, but I'll tell you what does. They're smart. Clever. Intelligent. They believe in instant communications, and have in fact been raised on it. And they have money. And they are very hard to pin down *because they don't want anything at all!*"

Jaca snatched up the petition again. "Read it. Read it carefully. *We* know that it is nothing but lies. The demands are meaningless — but they are *demands!*

They move in a different sense of reality than you or I or most adults our age. And they will use anything, anywhere, anytime, to create destruction —"

"But there must be something they want!" Coldwater said hoarsely.

"Anarchy," Jaca said. "Destroy. No discipline. No inner restraints. It's a demand by them for everything, and their only justification is that they are alive. They don't contribute anything. If you go into the Peace Corps, you're a square. If you want to join the Democratic or Republican parties, you're a square and a brown-nose."

"All right," Coldwater said, facing Jaca. "You know all about it."

"The patterns are the same — Cuba — Spain. The techniques are identical. The —"

"But you said they weren't Communists."

"I said the *patterns* were the same. As are the patterns in South Africa, suppressing the Blacks. Left and Right. It's the same method, but in this case to no specific end."

"They just want to destroy, is that it?"

"That's it," Jaca said. "And not all of them. Only a few. But it's hard to separate out the mere destroyers. There are legitimate issues to be gained. I don't blame them at all for wanting to throw out some old shit of a professor that spends most of his time reading the same lecture over and over again to each new class and spends his time writing books or lectures, or just sits and farts or picks his nose or gets drunk. Nor do I disagree with the Black militants who are forcing their way into what under our Constitution is rightfully theirs. What I am trying to explain to you, is that, without knowing the motives, you cannot negotiate."

"They don't want to negotiate, even if *I* wanted to."

"They'll negotiate," Jaca said. "That's about the only tangible thing they can achieve — sitting down on an equal basis with you and making themselves, their presence, felt and achieving in three days what has taken you a lifetime."

"It's all some kind of horrible mistake," Coldwater said.

"Then why don't you send in your sailors and crush them?" Jaca asked.

"They're kids. The Company, the ship — the publicity —"

"They know that as well as you. That's one of the things they're depending on. That you *won't* use the reality of harsh repressive measures against them."

"But — but you make it sound as if they were playing — a game — that doesn't have any rules."

Jaca smiled tiredly. He settled back and sipped his drink. "Isn't it? Isn't it a game they're playing without any rules, because the rules haven't been decided yet for this new and deadly exercise in *winning*?"

"Winning what?" Coldwater roared.

"That's the name of the game. Winning nothing. Losing nothing. With no rules. Just playtime. You know what they call it — the age of Aquarius."

"And what about their goddamn parents?" Coldwater demanded.

"It's too easy to blame the parents," Jaca said. "Remember, a parent — especially the father — is the same guy that has been working his ass off to build the nation and the economy. All he wanted was the best for his kids. And he slaved to get it."

"But why don't the parents knock hell out of them?"

"Simple, the parents, like you, don't know that the new game is winning nothing, losing nothing with no rules. They had things to win and lose and there were rules. And generally speaking, they didn't have much playtime either."

"Incredible. Absolutely in-fucking-credible." Coldwater nodded to himself several times. "All right. I'm not out to save the world and its patterns of behavior or cultural mores, I *am* concerned with my ship — what do you suggest?"

184

"Don't initiate action. React to what their next move will be."

"You think there's going to be more?"

"Much — much more. You're not dealing with a hardheaded bunch of drunken sailors, Abe, you've got a superior intelligence facing you and they have resources — resources powerful enough for you to back away from."

"What kind of resources?"

"The parents of some nineteen-year-old girl in tourist whom one of your sailors might bust in the mouth and damage all her teeth who are going to hold *you* responsible" — Jaca paused — "so you have to be on sure footing when you react." Jaca paused again. "Your ship, your career, and even disgrace, if you make a wrong move."

Captain Abraham Coldwater stared at Luis Jaca and could not, at that moment, believe that what was happening was happening, and that he was taking it all seriously.

Stern opened the door, followed immediately by Officer Joe Trapp. "Captain — excuse me, sir, but they've just invaded the first-class lounge. About a hundred of them —"

Jaca looked at Coldwater. "Be careful, Abe. Be very careful."

*　　*　　*

185

The invasion into the first-class lounge was only a diversion. Ralph Rome led a second group into the second-class theater where the movie was over and the theater empty and ripped every single seat and back and then quickly retired to the tourist deck.

The war had begun.

7

Colonel,
We Are Relating,
We're Relating Like Hell...

RALPH ROME had never been *very* good at anything. He was always good enough to make the football team, a pulling guard, never a back; to have his share of sort-of-pretty girls; to get his straight B-pluses; and although he really wanted a 740-cc Honda, he had to settle for a third-hand Mustang, which was useless for up-tight dates because of the automatic shift and the bucket seats, and which could not go into hiding under a shady tree as a Honda could. Ralph Rome was a clean-cut ordinary human being with no real talents and no clear idea of where he was going and no concern at all about the future.

But all that changed aboard the S.S. *New York*. With Indian in "that heavy vault" and out of the action, Rome was no longer *numero uno*, he was up on the skyline. He had, for the first time in his life, all the beautiful chicks he could want and no time to use them. He had and liked the security of the Midwest bike crowd and could not think of anything to send them to do. He was The Man. He was Mister Heavy. Everyone wanted to know what the echo was and where the action was going to hit next. He was protected. He was secure. He was listened to. And he didn't have an idea in his head about what to do, except what Indian had told him. He was happy, however, and the only thing that marred his newly acquired self-image was the fact that he didn't have a beard. He wore a beret, dark glasses, bush jacket, and suede boots with three-inch Spanish heels with a distinct flair. If he had had a beard, and dared to wear a .45, he would have been absolutely content.

But for all the things that Ralph Rome wasn't, for all the near-misses in his life, there was one thing that he was. He was an absolutely perfect executive officer, an administrator operating at command level.

Secure in his knowledge that all he would have to do was carry out Indian's orders, Ralph Rome was the ideal front man: *numero uno*. The overwhelming majority of the new coalition of freakies and squares accepted Rome as boss. Indian was something vague, and now out of it. They would get around to him in time, but for the moment, what's new, boss?

No one, with the exception of Cora Ingersoll who

knew a genuine action freak when she saw one, denied him his place or his orders. And it was Cora who recognized that, so far, the North Atlantic Students Redress Assembly had failed to come up with a genuine, straightforward and honest issue. The provocative items in the petition were fine for the initial galvanizing of the freakies and the squares, to get onto the boards, but there had to be something more solid, more devastating than complaints of bad food, vague accusations against Coldwater and demands for freedom of the ship. She studied the petition. She studied item three. Dr. Jaca. Indian had said he was the perfect patsy.

She remembered Elienne Peterson.

She considered for a moment, but only a moment, talking to Ralph Rome about her idea; she rejected that plan when she saw him hesitate over a decision. So far there had been no reaction from Coldwater to the theater destruction. Someone had suggested they hit again, this time in the first-class library. Ralph Rome had been unable to decide. Perhaps, he had countered, they should wait a little longer to see what Coldwater was going to do.

Cora Ingersoll made up her mind. She had to get to Indian.

It took some maneuvering, but by claiming that Indian was her half-brother she was able to speak to him through the peephole of the vault door while the chief master-at-arms stood to one side and listened.

"How are you?" Cora asked. "Are you all right?"

"I'm fine," Indian said, a little puzzled that she should make the effort to come see him. "I guess this will all be straightened out soon enough. I'd sure as hell hate to spend the rest of the trip in here, though." He frowned. "What's cooking?"

"Oh, nothing much. Some of those freaky kids tore up the theater in second class."

"Oh?" Indian was quick to keep the surprise and pleasure out of his voice. "That's kind of silly."

"I thought so too. I don't understand why they want to do things like that."

"Did you send a cable to Dad?" Indian asked innocently.

"Not yet. But I will soon as I get a chance. They won't let anyone near the radio room. It's fantastic. I mean, they've got guards all over the ship — it's horrible."

"Yeah," Indian said. "And otherwise, how are things?" He frowned.

"Well, you know, it's always better if you can separate them."

"Yeah," Indian said, picking up on her direction. "It is."

"I got to thinking about that poor Peterson girl. And that poor father, you know?"

"Yeah," Indian said, breathing quickly and with genuine approval of Cora. "Yeah, he must be busted out of his skull."

"It's horrible, I know, but I thought we — I mean, you know, some of the kids could send him flowers or something, you know to let him understand that it wasn't his fault."

"His?"

"Well, how would Dad feel if, for instance, it was me that was strung out and something happened to me in the hospital?"

"Yeah, he'd be up tight, all right," Indian said, nodding. "Yeah, I'd do that if I was you, you know. Send him some flowers and tell him how sorry we are, and you know, that item three was responsible, and in general that that's the way things are."

"Are you sure you're okay?" Cora asked again. "I mean, there isn't anything I can do for you, is there?"

"Get me out of here if you can," Indian said.

"There isn't anything I can do about that," Cora replied. "You want anything, like cigarettes or something?"

"No. Nothing. I'm okay."

"Well, I'll go — and send the flowers."

"Do that," Indian said.

The chief master-at-arms had listened and heard every word but dismissed it. He never understood what kids were talking about even when they talked directly to him. And besides, he wanted to get back to his novel. His eyes and attention had strayed several times during the conversation between the boy and the girl. He closed the peephole and gently but firmly escorted Cora out of the confined area, and hurried back to his book.

"Colonel Peterson?" Cora stood outside the door and looked up at the colonel, who stood, his face revealing nearly every emotion he felt, and stared at Cora. He was red-eyed and unshaven.

"What do you want?" he demanded.

"To talk to you if I may — to say things, you know, that I feel should be said to you." Cora nodded, as if affirming her own courage for coming there. "Please?"

"Come in." Peterson stood to one side and Cora passed into the cabin. Everything she hoped to see was there. The cabin was a mess. Colonel Peterson's grief was presented to her by the unshaven and distraught man, by the unmade bed, the clothes thrown carelessly around the cabin, a breakfast tray that was untouched, and a half-filled bottle of whiskey.

194

"Have you read our petition, Colonel?" Cora asked, standing in the middle of the mess.

"Yes."

"Item three?"

"About Dr. Jaca — yes."

"That's why I'm here, Colonel. To tell you that our petition is genuine and — if possible — to make a bridge between the communications of you and us. It isn't just here, aboard this ship, sir. It's everywhere —"

"Please, young lady, I'm not in the mood to listen to your speeches and not at all sympathetic to being recruited. And that's why you're here."

"Not at all, sir," Cora said quickly. "But I am here to tell you that what happened to Elienne —"

"Please leave."

"Colonel, please — you think you're any different from any other father in the same situation? What would my father feel if it were me down there in the icebox —" Cora paused. "I'm sorry, sir." She turned away as if to leave. She stopped. "I must tell you. Perhaps you are the —" She started to cry.

Colonel Algernon Peterson stood absolutely still.

"Why must there be such differences?" she said quietly. "I didn't even know your daughter. But yet, you know, I did. Because I've seen girls like her, too many of them, try to make up for something —"

Peterson did not move.

"— something that was missing between you — and us. I have the same problem with my own father."

"Young lady —"

"My name is Cora Ingersoll. I'm from Sandusky, Ohio. My father is an engineer with the county water department. And talking to you is just like talking to him."

"Miss Ingersoll. I don't know why you're here."

Cora turned, her face wet with tears. "I'm here because all of us, every last one of us, realize that, regardless of why we — Elienne, took acid, it might have been any of us. All right, all right, it was a foolish and stupid, really *stupid* thing to do, but it's done — and —"

"And what?" Colonel Peterson asked quietly.

"Once you knew about Elienne — once you knew — *really knew,* perhaps you could have tried to understand her, but you didn't get that second chance — they blew it, here, right here on this dumb boat!"

"Blew what?" Peterson asked.

"That creep — that doctor — every day, all over the world, kids like Elienne are dropping acid because they can't talk to their parents, or they don't know what to do about an up-tight, white-knight world; all they hear are the echoes from the past — your gossip about how hard it was, and all that stuff — and they drop the acid or they smoke pot or they do other things, but I never yet heard of a kid who had a bad trip getting killed from it!" Cora let her voice rise hysterically.

Peterson was rigid.

"You think we're action freaking just because we had rotten food? No! You're wrong. Elienne — *and I didn't know her* — might as easily been any one of us, and that's why we behave like we do, because we're told to go away and be good children. *We are not children — and neither was Elienne.*"

Cora turned and snatched the door open. "That's all I wanted to say, Colonel Peterson. That — that, we *know* about Elienne. And *we know what happened!*"

"*What* happened?" Colonel Peterson stepped forward. He almost grabbed her.

"Why don't you come down and listen to *our* side of it for a change!"

She dashed out.

The diversionary invasion of the first-class lounge was dispatched by the crew with almost no effort at all. There were a few passive resistors who were thrown bodily out onto the deck, but the rest of the sit-ins arose and left quickly and quietly.

Coldwater directed the whole operation. Heeding Jaca's advice, he would allow no overreaction by the crew. When he heard about the theater in second class and its destruction, which had included slashing the screen and the writing of four-letter words on the wall with lipstick, eyebrow pencil and felt-tipped pens, he controlled his rage as well as a man could, and started to deal as he saw best with the reality of Jaca's warnings. He sent Joe Trapp to find and locate the leaders with an offer to sit down and talk.

Ralph Rome was ready for him. Ling Jung, surrounded by security, arranged a meeting on the sun deck and demanded as the first order of business that Indian be released from the brig. There would be, Ling Jung said, no compromise on the point. Coldwater agreed to think about it.

"No," Ling Jung replied. "Now. We want an answer now."

"You're not going to get it," Coldwater said. "How do you like that?"

"How do you like the idea that the library in first class," Ling Jung said, "is going to be destroyed in one minute" — he glanced at his watch — "if Indian isn't released?"

Coldwater remembered the theater in second class, the destruction of the tourist salon and the tourist dining room. He faltered.

"Indian," Ling Jung said, whipping his fan of hair around. "You talk to Indian, and no one else."

"Granted," Coldwater said. He turned to Joe Trapp. "Release Indian. Bring him —"

"No!" Ling Jung said. "You don't *bring* him anywhere!"

Coldwater stared. He nodded. "Let him go."

"Shall we say at midnight, Captain? In the French Room?"

"For what?"

"Negotiations."

And while first- and second-class passengers watched and listened to the fantastic scene on the deck, Ling Jung, surrounded by his security, returned below to command headquarters and Ralph Rome.

Ten minutes later, no one was more surprised than Indian as he was returned to the tourist section, waving to the cheers and the shouts of victory from hundreds of students, taking it as easily as an astronaut returning from outer space, to find Colonel Peterson in deep conversation with Ralph Rome, Cora, Ugly and Fatso.

Indian looked at Cora and winked. "Good evening, Colonel," he said. "I'm very glad to see you here."

Colonel Peterson sat on one of the bunks in G-703 and looked at the circle of faces around him; red-eyed, bearded, long-haired, scruffy figures intent on their upcoming negotiations with Coldwater. They all but ignored him. This was a major meeting of the

Action Council and they were all there, Ugly, Fatso, Cora, Big Mouth, Ralph Rome, Ling Jung, with Film Maker recording it all, they watched and listened to Indian. The bike security was there, at their own insistence, taking their job very seriously. They were not going to let Colonel Peterson "throw a heavy hurt on our people again." They stood at one side in stolid confidence.

But Colonel Peterson was a very well-oriented man. He was not there now to fight back because of his personal grief over Elienne. He was genuinely impressed with the intelligence he heard in the conversation around him. He had exercised nearly all of his life a belief in the abstractions of the total rather than the individual unit soldier, and it was on this level that he was hoping to communicate. He was intelligent enough, and had been trained well enough, to dismiss their being so much younger than he (what about Alexander the Great, and William Pitt?) and he accepted the premise for the dialogue. And really, when he was in it, he could not help feeling profound respect for the way they were handling themselves and the situation.

Elienne was dead. There was nothing he could do about that. But there was much he could gain from learning about her — and them. He was embarking on a pragmatic learning process that was much like the world he had been trained to know; the killing ground, where you continued to advance even when your soldier buddy fell at your side. He embraced it with an abiding sense of comfort, moving forward, getting on with it. He studied Indian, and listened to him, trying to find the ring of some truth in the young man; but found nothing. It was like listening to a disembodied voice from a tape machine. There was nothing personal — Peterson hesitated to think of the right word — or *real* about him. There was no sign of the wild-eyed zealot, not a hint that a hot Communist was underneath that cool façade, not a suggestion of intellectual weakness as Indian spoke to the others in a calm and finely controlled voice, laying out ideas for the midnight meeting with Cold-water.

Colonel Algernon Peterson was keeping in mind something farther ahead in time: the supersecret war college buried in the heart of America where everyone, generals and lesser officers alike, wore plain clothes so that no one would be intimidated by rank, and ran their bull sessions day and night. He had already begun to build his own ready-answers so that he could back up his snap opinions (which would be anything but snap opinions) and explain to the one-, two- and three-star generals what was happening to A M E R I C A land of the free home of the brave, when after a lecture, he would have to go deeper into explaining his sharp questioning of the morning speaker. Peterson was aware of at least a half-dozen general officers who were still devoted to von Clauswitz's military-political theories. Now, at the Action Council meeting, almost with satisfaction, he thought, yes, this was what it was all about. The price he had had to pay to see it was Elienne. Well, so what? It was A M E R I C A, wasn't it? And wasn't America his duty? God, to have loved Elienne and then to have lost her.

Well, it was at least a way to get on with it. He looked at their faces. Who were they? What did they want? How were they going to get it? America was changing — *the world* was changing right before his eyes. One hundred and ninety-two years of constant, steady, recognizable growth and now this. But, as he looked and listened to *this,* he asked again, what *was* this? They were going to destroy the ship if they did not get what they wanted. They said it openly, plainly, right in front of him. He remembered France — he had been there in May and June, and he knew how it started. They would do it. He believed them. They would destroy the finest ship in the world. But what did they want? They themselves had said, and he had heard it a hundred times, that the left was dead, the radical left was even more of a disaster, and that Communism was a simplistic and boorish economic red-tape factory. But what else was there?

Colonel Peterson did not move a muscle. He was going to ride it right through. He was going to see if he couldn't get right to the bottom.

"Are you surprised that we let you know our plans, Colonel Peterson?" Indian asked.

"Not really," Peterson replied. "I don't think you'll let me out of here now."

"Well, in that sense, I guess you're right," Indian said quietly. He sat down on the deck and Cora immediately sat down beside him and put her head on his lap. They might have been, Peterson thought, looking at them, just home from a date or a football game. He dismissed the others. He concentrated on Indian.

"Can you tell me why?" the colonel asked.

"Why what?"

"Why are you doing it?"

"Oh, many reasons."

"I asked the same question of you once on deck, remember?"

"Yes, I do. I remember," Indian said.

"At that time you told me it was a concept of the waste of life."

"Accurate. That's what it is," Indian said.

"Please try to explain to me why it is now, suddenly, a waste of life, and old values are no longer regarded as meaningful."

"I can't speak for everyone, Colonel."

"Please pay me the respect of believing that my questions are honestly motivated and that I want to know and try to understand." Peterson's eyes bore into Indian, who stared back, coolly, as if he were making a dinner selection. "Don't be coy with me. I'm a military man and I appreciate every move you've made. You have my profound respect."

" 'Kay, Colonel," Indian said; he smiled. " 'Kay. In the first place, it's existential. Not any of that Sartre crap, but Camus, with the presences rolling over you."

Peterson nodded. "I understand the difference."

"Take that idea, and now hold it."

"All right."

"Now, we've tried it your way, Colonel," Indian said casually. "We've tried to stay with the system, you know? I mean, we've really tried it your way. But then there was the Jack Kennedy thing, murdered. Malcolm X, murdered. Then Martin Luther King, murdered. Then Bobby. Wiped out. Wasted. Now, I have to ask you, why that waste?"

"Political murders," Peterson said. "There are a lot of nuts wandering around."

"No, I don't accept that," Indian said. "It's the system. Your system. I also said to you up on deck that you hung on too long for the wrong things. And even so, we gave you another chance."

"By you, I take it you mean my generation?"

"Or anyone else who supports the system that can almost casually murder four magnificent men and then pray over them —" Indian shifted his weight. Cora nudged in closer. Looking at her, she was not unlike Elienne, Peterson thought. "— then turn around and demand, mind you, *demand,* that *we* continue to support that same system by going to Vietnam."

"You said you gave us another chance; what was that?"

"Senator McCarthy," Indian said. "Sucked in by the establishment and then wiped out."

"You can't blame everyone for what happened to the Kennedys and —"

"Then who, Colonel? Who? I mean, there's got to be somebody ready to do something —"

"And you're doing it?"

"Perhaps."

"The wrong way," Colonel Peterson said.

"But, *man!*" Indian said. "What is the *right* way?"

"You start by relating —"

"Colonel, we *are* relating. We're relating like hell all over the place. But you don't like our style of doing it."

"I don't call anarchy relating."

"It isn't anarchy," Indian said quickly. "It's action. And you know where most of us learned it, Colonel?"

"Where?" Colonel Peterson asked warily.

"At home. At the dinner table. In our schoolrooms. On our football fields. It's competition for this and win that and don't lose tonight, Johnny. And what does he win? More of the same useless material garbage that my mother and father worked like slaves to get. What about the spiritual things, Colonel? No room for that in the system? The humanities? So, you see, your competitions and your cut-throat system don't work for us. Why should we spend our lives building a better mouse-trap?"

"You don't have to. There's room in modern society for everyone."

"Except the Puerto Ricans. The Blacks. The North Vietnamese. The Jews. No, you're wrong again, Colonel Peterson. We've found something new. It's called action."

"Anarchy," Peterson said.

"*Total action.* And it works, Colonel, because until the last few years you didn't even know we were alive. But now, *now,* you're listening, baby. *You're listening!* You know we're alive because we've made a big enough noise, and we're going to continue to make big noises so that you will never forget us again. We're sick of your bombs, your power, your programs. Your ghosts walking around with IBM statistics — big ghosts, little ghosts — all directing our lives, our future; who are they, Colonel Peterson? Who are the ghosts and where do they live?"

"With a society as complicated as ours, you find a redundancy in names for individuals, and numbers are infinite, so —"

"To hell with numbers. What have numbers got to do with a man's life?"

"Numbers are impersonal."

"Exactly," Indian said with that sudden flashing and charming smile. "Exactly."

"All right," Peterson said. "You need something more personal. I don't object to your search, I object to your methods, how's that?" Peterson looked at Indian. "Is that a fair statement?"

"It's only a half-truth, Colonel," Indian said. "What about the other half?"

"What other half?"

"The half that puts *us* under *your* influence. And you won't listen to what we have to say."

"I'm listening now. I've tried very hard — for personal reasons, and for professional reasons — to understand you. I object to your methods."

"But your rules of behavior and conduct won't allow us entry into seats of power, where the ghosts make decisions for us! So we have developed action —"

"But it's meaningless action, from what I can see. What is there to gain by destroying this fine ship?"

"You said it earlier, Colonel. It's called relating. We burn down a building on a college campus, we tear up paving stones on the streets of Paris, we fight Russian tanks in Prague — we destroy a fine ship. It's called relating. It's the only thing left to us. You've jammed us up, and put very heavy burdens on us, like wars, and sociological norms, and psychological tests to stuff us into neat pigeonholes, which by the way follow us the rest of our lives. Let one kid smack another kid in the eye in the yard at recess and he gets a mark on his chart that says Johnny is antisocial. Then when he goes to get a job, the IBM card trots it out and there you are, you're antisocial. No job. Your military establishment is quite famous for that fitness report."

"But if —" Colonel Peterson was getting closer to the bottom of it now. He felt he could carry it through and he wanted to know. He really wanted to know. "But if I don't accept your premise that what you call action is relating, then what?"

"Then you have what you call anarchy."

"Or war," Peterson said quietly.

208

"That's something you understand, isn't it?" Indian said.

"When there is something to win."

"Kill the enemy?" Indian asked.

"To maintain society, yes, if need be."

"Are we the enemy, Colonel?"

"Are you?" Colonel Algernon Peterson looked Indian in the eye.

"No," Indian said slowly, returning the stare, "but we might become the enemy if you and your people don't stop yo-yoing us around."

"That sounds dangerously close to being a threat — a blackmail threat," Peterson said.

"It is," Indian said simply. "But as you know, a threat is only effective if the threatening party is capable of carrying it out. I think that in a half-dozen countries there has been ample demonstration that we *can* carry out the threat."

"And become the enemy," Peterson said slowly.

"And become the enemy. You'd like to slap us down right now, but you can't do it without guns, Mace. You sure as hell can't dig out those old slogans anymore." Indian paused. "Can you, Colonel?"

"Then you're talking — revolution."

"But not one you can put down, quite so easily, with guns. You can't exterminate the compulsions of youth."

"Is there any way to avoid what you imply is inevitable?" Peterson asked.

"Just listen to us," Indian said. "That's all. Just listen to our side of it."

"Take orders?"

"That really hurts you, doesn't it? Yes, Colonel, if the idea is good, and the point is made, then why not?"

"Then you would be the next General of the Army and I would be —"

"On the outside," Indian said quietly. "Like we are now."

"I understand now," Peterson said. "It really comes right back to the basic concepts of holding power."

"I thought you understood that at the beginning," Indian said with a quick smile. "Of course, it's all power, Colonel, but —"

"But?"

"Whose?"

Before the colonel could respond, the door opened and one of the bike security slipped inside. His face was flushed. He had a high color. "We're ready," he said to Indian.

Six of the bike security and Cora stood up instantly and as Indian turned back to the colonel, who waited, watching them, Indian spoke almost casually. "Would you like to see something, Colonel Peterson?"

"What?"

"Do I have your word that you won't interfere?"

"Is it going to involve violence?"

"No," Indian said.

"Then you have my word."

"Just do as I say, please."

By twos and threes the whole group left the cabin. Indian and Colonel Peterson walked side by side with bike security ahead of them and behind them. The companionways were teeming as usual: no one noticed them. At a junction of the stairs and elevators, the party split, with Cora and several of the bike security taking the elevator. Indian removed his headband and combed his hair back and slipped on a pair of shades, and Peterson was amazed at how this minor change altered Indian's appearance. They took the stairs. Moving as easily as in a crowd emptying from a ballpark after a game, the bike security, Indian and Peterson passed along the companionways of second and first class and made their way up and down through a maze of public rooms and companionways; Peterson did not ask any questions nor did he speak.

He just followed and observed Indian, having no idea where they were going or what they were going to do, until they arrived at the radio room. He saw Cora then, standing at the desk making out a form, talking to the telegrapher then on duty. Several of the bike security that had accompanied her stood to one side reading the cable forms.

On a signal from Indian, Ralph Rome appeared from around a corner, and the bike security at the desk moved in on Cora, took her from behind, yoking her, holding her mouth as Rome approached the desk without breaking stride. He spoke to the telegrapher in a low calm voice. "I want to use your radio. If you don't let me, we'll kill her."

"But — but —" the telegrapher objected.

To one side Colonel Peterson watched, stunned and angry, and would have made a move if it had not been for the bike security on either side of him, and for the fact that, at that moment, Indian turned and looked at him, removing his glasses and staring coolly into the colonel's eyes. "You gave your word, Colonel," Indian said calmly.

Ralph Rome vaulted over the desk lightly and forced the telegrapher back into the inner room where banks of radio equipment filled every available inch of space. The door was left open and the bike security, still holding the struggling Cora, followed Ralph Rome and the telegrapher into the room. The door closed.

It had all happened so fast that the few passing passengers did not notice there was anything wrong. Colonel Peterson stared at the door. He could not take his eyes from it. Indian's bike security were casual, but they watched Colonel Peterson intently. If he made a move or tried to sound an alarm, they were ready. Neither Indian nor Peterson said a word as they waited. It did not take long, but the few minutes that did pass seemed like an eternity to Peterson. Eventually he was even able to take his eyes from the door and stare at Indian. His color returned. He sighed. He let his whole body relax. He had come to learn. He was learning.

The radio room door opened and Cora was the first to leave. She did not look at Indian or any of the bike security, but simply slipped around a corner and was gone. A moment later, Ralph Rome came out of the door. He looked around, spotted Indian and nodded, then, following Cora's example, he walked casually past Indian and Peterson without even looking at them. The last to leave were the bike security, and they too just walked away. There was no alarm, no noise, nothing in fact but a temporarily empty service desk at the radio room and the closed door of the radio room itself.

Indian turned to Peterson, sighed, smiled and handed him a slip of paper. The bike security around

them just walked away and left the two men standing by the deserted radio desk.

"My God, you really took over the radio communications," Peterson said, looking at Indian. "For what
reason?"

"Read it, Colonel," Indian said. "All we needed to
do was send out one message. The one you have in
your hand. The whole world is waiting and listening
now."

"For what?"

"Us," Indian said simply. "Read it, Colonel."

Colonel Peterson opened the paper. It was a type-
written message:

TO THE ENTIRE WORLD THE NORTH ATLANTIC STU-
DENTS REDRESS ASSEMBLY HAS RESISTED CRIMINAL
EFFORTS BY CAPTAIN ABRAHAM COLDWATER TO EN-
FORCE INHUMAN TREATMENT ABOARD THE S.S. NEW
YORK CURRENTLY AT SEA. SIXTEEN HUNDRED STU-
DENTS HAVE SUCCESSFULLY MAINTAINED THEIR
PHYSICAL WELL-BEING BY TAKING CONTROL OF THE
SECOND CLASS AND TOURIST CLASS SECTIONS OF THE
SHIP AND ARE AT PRESENT NO LONGER IN DANGER.
TO THE ENTIRE WORLD. LISTEN! THIS IS NOT A
MUTINY. NO ATTEMPT WILL BE MADE TO SEIZE
CONTROL OF THE SHIP, OR INTERFERE IN ANY WAY
WITH THE DIRECTION OR THE PROGRESS TO NEW
YORK. THE NORTH ATLANTIC STUDENTS REDRESS
ASSEMBLY HAS BY ITS ACTIONS PREVENTED THE
SYSTEMIZED SUPPRESSION OF HUMAN RIGHTS AND

HAS RESISTED AS ALL STUDENTS AROUND THE
WORLD ARE RESISTING DECEIT, HYPOCRISY AND
LYING COMPROMISE. PEACE. . . . V

Colonel Peterson read and reread the message. He
looked up. Indian was looking at him with a flat,
unemotional expression. He saw no triumph there,
no sense of victory, there was not the slightest hint of
a vengeful, rhapsodic savoring of sweet success. Indian watched him with that cool indifference Peterson had come to associate with the young man. "It's
stunning," Peterson said. "Even brilliant."

Indian reached out and took the paper from the
colonel and calmly tore it up. "I have to leave, Colonel, you understand," Indian said. "Get away from
here."

"I'll go with you."

Indian shrugged and turned, walking away to the
nearest door and the outside deck. They said nothing.

Once outside, Indian dropped down several decks,
moving quickly and like a shadow to the safety of the
boat deck. There he stopped and leaned on the railing. He removed the shades and put his headband
back on. He let the wind blow in his face. Peterson
stood beside him.

"What happens now?"

"Depends," Indian said quietly. "We've made our
point."

215

"Depends on what?"

"Captain Coldwater."

"Of course," Peterson said, breathing a little more easily, taking it in, absorbing it, tasting it; he was a man who knew the essence of victory. "Will you tell me what your projection is?"

"What projection?"

"You have alternatives?"

"Only the basic psychology of predictable behavior."

"Coldwater's?"

"He's been taken. Wiped out."

Peterson thought of the message again. "Yes, you've won. But the alternatives — what if he reacts —"

"Do you mean overreact?" Indian asked quietly.

"That's what I mean. What then?"

"He can only get himself in deeper," Indian said casually. "He has to live with it now, doesn't he?"

"Unfortunately, yes," Peterson said.

"Put yourself in his position, Colonel," Indian said. "What would you do?"

"I don't know. I honestly don't know."

Indian waved his hand. It was a simple private gesture. Eloquent, speaking without words. There was nothing that *could* be done.

8

It's Something
That Is So Pure—
So Clean—So Definitive
That It Doesn't Even
Have a Name...

NEWS OF THE SEIZURE of the ship's radio coursed through the great vessel within minutes after the fact. Mimeographed copies of the message appeared and were handed from passenger to passenger, who read the declaration with a quickening sense of dread. The crew reacted with stunned outrage. Many passengers abandoned all pretense at having a good time and took to their cabins and suites. They wanted to have the voyage over with. The acrid odor of chaos permeated their solid sense of security and fun, and like birds before a coming hurricane, they retreated into hiding. The disappointment they had felt at having their voyage interrupted by the students' antics was now galvanized into distrust of Captain Coldwater, even borderline hysteria. A current of fear developed rapidly, and reached a crest at nine o'clock when there was not one single customer

in the French Room. There was not one single occu-
pant in the first- and second-class theaters. Less than
one hundred diners were at the cabaret, and of these,
the majority were sympathetic students who happened to be traveling in first and second class. There
was a fantastic demand for room service that night.
The ordinary frantic rush at meal hour was tripled
by the demands of the barricaded passengers. A
hundred different stewards and waiters were told to
leave the food wagons and trays outside the doors.
The great vessel was silent. Despite the locked-in,
tightened-up security the shipboard mood was chilly,
unquiet and portentous.

But beyond the great ship, in a dozen capital cities,
newscasts on television and radio interrupted regu-
larly scheduled programs to flash the word. The
world was already weary of a daily routine of real or
puffed-up dramatics; but this was something different. Almost immediately the ship was besieged with
cablegrams to husbands, wives, mothers, fathers,
business associates and offspring aboard. Captain
Coldwater spent two hours on the telephone with the
Company officials assuring them that everything was
under control. At eleven-thirty, he called a meeting
in his quarters of all officers of the luxury liner.

"I don't give a good goddamn for anything but my
ship! The meeting with the students is canceled. No

negotiations." Captain Abraham Coldwater stood in the middle of his sitting room and waved his hands at the assembled officers. "That's the last goddamn straw, you hear me! The last! I am not, repeat, I am not a goddamn Captain Bligh. I command the finest ship that ever floated on God's oceans and I am not, *not — goddamn not —* going to let a handful of snotnose kids take over my radio communications and put out this mindless garbage about me and my crew. *Now, that's the goddamn word, gentlemen!* If this ain't mutiny, then I don't understand the meaning of the word. I'm justified in anything and everything I do to protect my passengers, crew and ship cargo in that order. And if one of those slimy kids gets in my way, then it's too goddamn bad for him. Now hit the goddamn decks, Misters, and let 'em know what's what and who's who. Mr. Trapp!"

"Sir!"

"This is a direct order. Go below, use whatever manpower you need and confine 'em to quarters. They eat in shifts of one hundred, fifteen minutes each. Any sonofabitch that doesn't listen, or do as you say, then make him do as you say. We ain't on no goddamn campus now, and I don't give a damn if the whole world *is* watching, this is the high seas and *I'm God.* And you'd better believe it, and I'm telling you what to do."

"Yes, sir." Joe Trapp reached for his hat. "Let's go, Chief." He pointed his finger in a supreme gesture of authority at the chief master-at-arms.

Captain Coldwater turned to his desk and grabbed up the phone. "Where the hell are we!" he demanded. "All right, call the engine room and tell 'em I said I want every goddamn inch of turn they can get outa the screws, and I want it now!"

He slammed down the phone. Jaca stood with Joe Trapp at the door. "Captain —"

"What the hell is it?" Coldwater demanded.

"Captain," Jaca said, "you're playing right into their hands."

"To hell with it," Coldwater said, his face full of hate and frustration. "Mr. Trapp, I gave you an order."

"Captain —" Jaca tried again.

"Mr. Trapp!"

"If you go down there," Jaca said desperately, "you're doing the wrong thing!"

"Dr. Jaca," Coldwater bellowed. "This is not your area of discipline."

"Give in to them, Captain," Jaca pleaded. *"There's nothing for you to gain!"*

"I can show them what it means to go against the command and authority of the sea!" Coldwater roared.

"It's too late for that."

"Dr. Jaca!"

"They've made their case, Captain," Jaca said desperately. "Are you so damn dumb that you can't see that you've been had!"

"Dr. Jaca!"

"Abe, Abe," Jaca pleaded desperately, "listen to me. The whole world knows now. That's all they wanted. What more can they do? What more do they want? Nothing. They've achieved what they set out to do. Carefully, building up an issue out of lies and maneuvers, they've already got enough against you to make the whole world seriously listen to them and to question your judgment. Can't you see that they have already won! And if you send Trapp below to give them a roughhouse, they'll fight back. And they will, Abe."

"I hope to Christ they do," Coldwater said. "I hope to sweet Christ there is one, just one that will fight back."

"You don't know what you're talking about, man!" Jaca yelled. "If you leave 'em alone, the burden of proof for their actions will be on them. They will have to justify their actions until now — but even then I doubt it. What are you going to do with sixteen hundred of them, with their parents waiting on the pier to take their innocent children home with them and get them away from the bigoted, surly, hard-handed master of the sea! Huh! Think, goddammit, *think!* They will have to prove that the food was rotten, that I was incompetent, that your behavior was criminal — and where did they get the mimeograph paper and machine? If you're so angry that you can't see that you only have another day before you get to *your resources,* then perhaps you shouldn't be commander of the finest ship afloat.

"But if you send Trapp down there to give them a hard time, Abe, I swear to you, the early lies, the created incidents — which you have a chance now of tracking down and nailing them for what they are — they'll vanish. All that will be seen and heard will be the fight, and it *will* be a fight, Abe, they will fight back with everything they have. And when it's all over with, Abe, *listen to me!* They will disperse, and walk away from it without a backward glance! As long as they are aboard, restricted in a closed community, they represent a power, but the minute you get to New York, their power dissolves and their individual lives take over — their parents, their schools, *their other world.* But right now they're having the time of their lives, and there isn't anything they'd like better than to divide this ship up into two armed camps. One yours and one theirs.

"And then," Jaca said, looking at all of the officers,

"when you get to New York, what can you do with sixteen hundred of them!"

Captain Coldwater was listening. There was a distinct and very obvious difference in the vibration of the ship. Only those who heard Coldwater give the order knew that the ship was increasing speed.

"I can arrest the leaders now," Coldwater said. "That one they call Indian, and a few others."

"You've already seen what good that did," Jaca said. "They have, I am sure, a contingency plan for just such action as that."

"Like what?" Coldwater asked.

"Like refusing to leave the ship unless all of them leave the ship," Jaca said. "And if you send Trapp down there now, all you will do is harden up that resolve. Leave 'em alone, Abe. Ride it out. Only a day more from New York. Let 'em go, and before you know it, and I swear it will happen, they'll be out on deck with their guitars, singing, maybe taunting the crew or trying to provoke incidents, but it will have been over and the closer we get to New York, the more fragmented they will become."

"You're asking me to give up my authority," Coldwater said slowly.

"No, I'm not. I'm asking you to refrain from inciting a riot — one that you cannot win except by the most primitive and brutal methods, and that will never be understood by the thirty-two hundred —"

"*What* thirty-two hundred?" Coldwater asked.

"Parents," Jaca said.

Captain Coldwater paced the deck a few turns and looked at his men. He turned and looked back at Jaca. He thought for a moment of making an appeal to his officers, taking a vote, but his instinct and training would not allow him to consider that. There was the always present awareness of how long and how hard it had been to arrive at his present command. The decision was his. He could not diminish it by asking for opinions. Everything Jaca had said was true. Insurance would cover the damage. The Company's public relations firm would handle any of the tougher decisions. Once in New York he could draw, as Jaca had pointed out, on his own resources.

Stern knocked on the door and entered. His face was ashen. He looked at Captain Coldwater. "Sir, one of the watch A.B.'s is here."

"All right," Coldwater said.

A tall hard-muscled sailor entered the sitting room. He swiped at his watch cap and looked around the room. He licked his lips. "Cap'n, sir."

"Pricehouse, isn't it?" Coldwater said, recognizing one of his older hands.

"Yes, sir. Sir, they're —" Pricehouse stopped. He looked around at the officers again. "They're — there's about a hundred of them smoking pot and swimming —" Pricehouse stopped again. "Swimming naked in the first-class pool, sir." He stopped again. "Boys and girls, sir — *they're fucking!*"

Coldwater shifted his gaze and looked at Jaca. The two men stared at each other across the gulf of a shattered appeal to reason. Jaca slumped. He turned to the door. "I'd better get the dressing station set up," he said quietly.

"Trapp!" Coldwater said harshly.

"Sir?"

"Clean 'em out."

"Yes, sir."

Sir Harry and Lady Weldon had ignored the secretive, almost conspiratorial air that had invaded the great ship, and after dinner had decided to take a stroll around the deck. Sir Harry had paused momentarily to light his pipe and Lady Weldon had continued to walk on ahead to the railing overlooking the first-class pool. She stopped. She stared at what surely must be her imagination. But no, it wasn't. It was real. Below her, the laughing swimmers were all nude. A dozen couples were making love. "Harry," she said softly, speaking over her shoulder, "I think you should see this. It's really quite — yes, quite fantastic. Do you remember your Dante?"

"Yes, of course, what about it?" He stared over the railing. He dropped his pipe. "My dear," he said in a quavering voice. "I don't think we should stay."

"Harry," Lady Weldon said softly, "why do they behave in this manner?"

"I don't know — I don't — it's beyond the realm of my experience. I just — don't think that way."

"Of course not, my dear — how could you," Lady Weldon said. She turned from the railing and they continued their stroll. "You're a civilized man."

"Thank you, my dear," Sir Harry said, still quavering.

"There's a madness in the air," Lady Weldon said. "It's as if something evil had risen out of the underworld. A dark, misting shade, all powerful, that could destroy everything. Do you remember the night when we were in the winter islands?"

"And you heard the voodoo drums?" Sir Harry said. He suddenly felt very old and tired.

"Yes, that night. The drums were something we couldn't relate to, something we couldn't understand, and that's the way I feel now."

Their quiet, lonely walk was interrupted by sudden shrieks and screams as Trapp's men invaded the pool area. Lady Weldon stopped. They both stared back at the railing, and the lights of the pool beyond and below. Screams, hoarse shouts, oaths, crashes and yells spilled over one another. Flickering shadows rose from the filtered light of the pool and raced back and forth. She gathered her shawl closer around her shoulders. Sir Harry circled his wife with a protective arm. They both stood immobile and watched the shadows and listened to the violence. The thick and ugly sound of flesh being struck became counterpoint to the wilder yells and screams. And as quickly as it had happened, it was over. They were left standing as before, staring back at the filtered light of the pool and heard no other sound except the wash of the ocean against the skin of the ship.

"Surely this is the madness of hell," Lady Weldon breathed.

It may or may not have been the madness of hell, it depended entirely on your point of view, but the naked, bruised and bloodied girls and boys were herded coldly below into the tourist section much like lost souls into the eternal pit. And this aroused a new form of madness among the students. And as Indian had predicted, the S.S. *New York* was turned into a battlefield that night.

The first major engagement was fought in the companionway outside of G-703 when two dozen of Trapp's sailors attempted to confine Indian and the Action Council to quarters. The bike security responded with a curiously professional cold-blooded attack, successfully resisted the invasion and declared the companionway off-limits to anyone not checked out and cleared by Ralph Rome. The sailors didn't have a chance.

229

Slowly, in widening circles, like a gigantic family fight in which one and then another of the family is drawn into the contest, a half-dozen different areas became war zones. The tourist section became the focal battleground as Trapp attempted to seal off the lower decks. Vicious skirmishes were fought as the students resisted the suppressive tactics of Trapp and his sailors. Individual leaders emerged from the student body, many of them — like Winston Beauchamp and Joe Kazzipi — not at all associated with the North Atlantic Students Redress Assembly but driven by the collective front of Trapp and his sailors into a solid coalition; and time and time again, like World War II partisans, the individual bands merged until there was a solid army. Under the direction of Ralph Rome, who was guided by Indian through Cora, a general attack was launched by students against sailors on various decks and in different parts of the ship.

The French Room saw a battle that sustained itself for nearly an hour. Two hundred students fought back with water hoses of their own, with chair legs of their own, and in fact set the pace for violence. A fire resulted, accidentally, and in a half-hour the French Room was gutted. Trapp had no alternative but to turn his attention to the fire and leave the students to regroup and hit sailors' lines at

another point. The fire was quickly handled by the
experienced seamen, but nevertheless caused panic
among the passengers and forced Coldwater to declare a general emergency. He armed his officers and
petty officers and stationed guards on the darkened
deck at each lifeboat, and then took personal command of the ship's forces in the war against the
students.

Not all of the passengers in first and second class
remained in their cabins, in spite of the fact that it
was past midnight. Sickened and outraged at the
behavior of the students, many joined the sailors in
their fight against the ravaging bands that roamed
the ship. The students did not seem to care what the
risks were: they ripped and plundered, and in every
compartment they entered they wrought destruction.
Bedding, furniture, equipment were torn and
smashed and thrown over the side. The tourist salon
was fired, and when it got out of control the students
themselves fought the blaze.

At dawn the ship was still pounding at its greatest
speed toward New York. The blue, white, gold, red
and black of the superstructure was spotted with the
scorch marks from the fires. And trailing in the wake
of the great vessel, bedding, tables, chairs, luggage
left a watery waste of evidence to the destruction.

And even at dawn, it did not pause. The students

with unabated rage pursued their revenge for the swimming pool carnage. Both sides sustained heavy casualties. On his own, Jaca had sent Nurse Carol through the battle lines with medical supplies to care for the sick and injured among the students; and in an absurd moment the fighting stopped, and Nurse Carol, accompanied by three sailors with supplies, was passed through the lines and given every courtesy as she set up a dressing station in the tourist dining room. Then the lines were redrawn, a second breath caught, and the battle resumed with a renewed violence and vigorously sustained pace. To the trained eyes of Colonel Peterson, who was much more interested in the tactics of the students than in the sailors, there was not one wrong move. It was one of the most classic lines of defense, then attack, then fall back, probe and attack again, that he had ever encountered. And when he stopped to consider that it was done without any real overall leadership, but much of it by gut instinct and reaction, he saw that truly these were the enemy. He did not have the slightest idea where or when a battle such as he was witnessing might take place in America, but he was aware that many such battles had already taken place in cities around the world — Prague — Paris — Barcelona — Montevideo; and that the May–June riots in Paris had spread to a massive nationwide general strike and it could happen in America. He recognized immediately the basic superior intelligence of the students. And on a dozen different occasions he witnessed them facing terrible situations, which they easily and quickly dealt with by translating them into the abstractions of the football field, the geometry of tennis, the pure and violent art of lacrosse.

If Indian was the leader of them all, there were many individual group leaders who would hit and run, hit and run, with forces just large enough to maintain a general line of defense; the students did not really occupy the ship so much as control sections of it in classic guerrilla fashion, like Tito in Yugoslovia and the Viet Cong in Vietnam.

The students had secured the lower decks of the tourist section and had successfully taken over the main lounges of the second-class section. They were pressing their attacks with superior forces and energy, with vastly superior risk-taking capacity and finally with a superior use of psychology; they would hold a line, then detach members to strike out at a totally new and vulnerable section of the ship. The entire crew had now joined the battle. Maids, cooks, stewards, sailors, oilers, wipers, clerks and typists. By 10 A.M. on the morning of the last day at sea, three-quarters of the ship was in the hands of the students and they were pressing forward. All that remained were the crew quarters, the bridge, engine room and the boat deck. Both sides had been fighting all night. Three thousand five hundred people were exhausted, sickened, disgusted, insane with fear and anger, hungry for revenge yet completely without resources to think, to reason, to find a way out of the absolutely absurd situation. Both sides prayed that the ship would get to New York and that it would be over.

It could not last much longer. But it did. The dynamic of the battle was such that it could not easily be slowed or stopped. Lines of communication on both sides began to break down. Discipline among Coldwater's sailors had shattered. Individual officers and their men ceased to function according to the time-honored laws of the sea; years of rigidity were swept aside as groups of sailors refused to pull back on orders by their officers, and this caused a complete breakdown in command and a reversion to the laws of survival and revenge. The students countered this development with resourceful tactics of their own: they simply started taking prisoners. The sailors imitated them. Students taken by the sailors were held in the first-class gym, while sailors taken by the students were held in cabins on F Deck, with the bike security validated as warders.

234

By 1 P.M. Jaca was near to dropping with exhaustion and when he heard from the wounded who came to him that there was to be an exchange of prisoners, he thought surely he was completely out of his mind. But he saw that the act, the thought of the act, however absurd, was the one reasonable thing that had happened since the war had begun. If the fighting was to stop for the incredible event of Coldwater and Indian exchanging prisoners, it might be just the moment to make an appeal to both sides.

Colonel Peterson had, throughout the night and morning, refused absolutely to take part in the battle between crew and students. Even when many of the first- and second-class passengers joined the crew, he did not allow himself to get involved. He remained above it all. Mostly he was behind the crew's lines — but twice he was caught behind the students' lines when they had executed some brilliant maneuver and he was trapped, only to be allowed to go where he wanted.

He observed. He stored up knowledge. He began to form his remarks to the generals at the war college. He took notes. He was totally committed to the idea that the students were enemies of the United States. He had already begun to form several basic concepts on how to deal with the coming revolution. The officer corps of the Military in the United States had always drawn on the college students, through the reserves and ROTC, to form the backbone and flesh out their ranks in times of emergency, but this would not be the case now. The students would be on the other side. And they were good. They would be a formidable enemy.

It could not last much longer. But neither side would cease to press every advantage that appeared. At last at three o'clock there came a lull: both sides had fought themselves into complete exhaustion. The flow of the injured arriving at Jaca's dressing station began to slow down. No food had been served — or even prepared to his knowledge — since the previous day. Jaca knew he would have a serious health problem if something didn't give soon. When a young deckhand appeared at the dressing station with a badly sprained wrist swollen to twice its normal size, Jaca was given information that made his hands shake.

"They're already to the main lounge in first class that leads directly to the boat decks," the sailor reported to Jaca. "I guess they'll get them next — and then it's the bridge." He writhed in pain as Jaca set and taped the wrist. Jaca gave him a sedative. "Whatever happens after this," Jaca told him, "you're out of it."

236

"No I ain't, Doc, I'm gunna get me some of that long hair and love beads. You can't stop me. You oughta've seen what they did to an ordinary on my watch. They beat him —"

The sailor jumped from the dressing table and hurried back to the battlefront, which at that time had worked its way up both starboard and port sides of the ship to the first-class lounge, with the crew's forces fighting with their backs forward and the students rising up out of the lower decks from the stern.

"Take over, Kenneth," Jaca said. The young nurse looked at him.

"Dr. Jaca, don't go up there."

"Did you hear what that sailor said?" Jaca said quietly. "They're in the first-class lounge — next to the boat deck and the lifeboats."

"Doctor, let 'em do what they want to. It ain't our fight. Jesus! Ain't it enough that we bandage them after they — their craziness?"

"No, it isn't, Kenneth. Take over. If they go for the boats, Captain Coldwater has every right in the world to shoot them down."

"Well, let him! Goddamn 'em." The young nurse's face was drained of color. "I used to see guys like this at school, you know, always yelling and hollering. And what the fuck do they know! Nothing. They couldn't wipe their own ass if it wasn't for their mamas and papas. Wait'll they get out in the world, out'na jungle and find out that a body isn't worth a good goddamn unless they can show a hundred cents on the dollar of goods and services delivered for the dinero they take home. Let 'em fall for some sweet young chick and after the first six months' fucking is over, then let 'em go and see what it's all about in the great big bad world —"

Jaca stood at the door and listened. It was a point of view. It was a cry of honest outrage. There were no abstractions in Kenneth's arguments. It was a good, honest gut reaction. And moment for moment, day for day, year for year, the Kenneths of the world were infinitely more valuable to society than the subsidized overeducated idiots who were destroying the ship.

"Leave it alone, Kenneth," Jaca said.

"Leave what alone!" Kenneth yelled. He stood over a very old sailor who had sustained a bad cut on his chest when he had been struck with a metal chair. "You can bet your sweet ass, Dr. Jaca, that when it comes time to pay off they can't cut it. They just can't. And there are a hell of a lot of us that didn't go to Harvard or Yale — did you know that I have a theory of nerve fibrosis? Did you? No, you didn't, *because I'm a mustang!*"

"Take it easy, kid," the old sailor said.

"Fuck you too." Kenneth said. "And if you don't like it, then shove it —"

"What about your theory of nerve fibrosis?" Jaca asked.

"Fuck it!" Kenneth said.

"And that's the difference," Jaca said quietly. "If they had an idea for nerve fibrosis, they wouldn't let go of it; but you're so hung up on being a, what was it you called it, a mustang? — that you can't see they would accept honesty when it is found, character when it is found. The only difference is that they don't have to worry about money, family, tradition —"

"And merit!" Kenneth screamed at him.

"Take it easy, kid!" the old sailor said. "You're hurting me."

Jaca turned away from the dressing station and hurried up to the upper decks. He worked his way forward on the second-class C Deck to the forward elevators to get behind the crew's lines before he went topside. The elevator door opened and he was face to face with Gloria Sheaffer.

"Jaca —" She hesitated.

"You should be in your suite," Jaca said.

"I couldn't stay in there any longer. I had to do

239

something — something — help — something, but not hide. Jaca. What's it all about?"

"It's something that is so pure — so clean — so definitive that it doesn't even have a name."

"I mean the students —"

A chair flew past them. There was a loud scream and in the companionway to their right a sailor suddenly appeared, and there it was, all of it, wrapped up in one sailor being felled by a thrown chair. The sailor retreated, rushing past Gloria and Jaca, and only a second later two students came chasing after him. The expressions on their faces turned Jaca into stone. They moved with sureness. Jaca reacted instantly. He shoved Gloria into the elevator and pressed the button closing the door, at the same time turning to face the advancing students. They came forward inexorably. One carried a chair leg. Jaca felt the presence of someone in back of him. He whirled.

Colonel Peterson stood shoulder to shoulder with him. "I'll take the one with the chair leg," Peterson announced calmly.

Jaca nodded. They started to advance together. The two students, who began to back up, retreated several steps, then turned and ran, disappearing around the corner into the companionway.

"Thank you," Jaca said. "I didn't realize they had penetrated quite this far."

"I think it's very nearly over," Peterson said dryly. "There are few areas that I can find they don't control."

"No," Jaca said, studying the colonel. "It's not quite over yet."

Peterson looked at him. "What do you mean?"

"If they get to the lifeboats, Coldwater is going to start shooting. He has to."

Peterson studied the doctor for a long moment. Then he nodded slowly. "Of course. He would have to."

"Do you know what that would mean?"

"I think so."

"I'm on my way to find him now and try to convince him to surrender — to let them have it their way — to keep it from becoming murder."

Peterson said nothing.

"Will you come with me? Your presence might lend weight in an area."

"What area?"

"An appeal to reason for lack of a better way of saying it. Something has to be done to stop this insanity." Jaca took a deep breath. Peterson seemed to hesitate. Jaca turned away and pushed the button for the elevator.

"Why wasn't it stopped before?" Peterson asked.

"Why wasn't any war stopped before it happened? Stupidity. Lack of foresight. Indecision. The preservation of the status quo. The lust for power. Many reasons, Colonel."

"You think this is a war?"

"I think," Jaca said tiredly, feeling his fatigue more than he had ever felt it before in his life, "that this is only the beginning of a world crisis. It won't be isolated to the Western world either. The other side of the moral and political fence had better take heed."

Colonel Peterson nodded very slowly. He turned away and took a few steps in the corridor near the elevators. "I went hunting in northern Canada once," Peterson said. "We tracked for a week and a half and finally found our herd of caribou. We wounded an old bull, but before we could get to him to finish him, a wolf pack had gotten to him. But the adult wolves were not attacking. They hung back and let the wolf cubs get their first taste of the kill —" Peterson looked at Jaca. "That's the situation now, isn't it, with Indian and Coldwater?"

"You understand it all," Jaca said quietly.

The elevator door opened. Gloria Sheaffer rushed out. She was very cool, very, *very* cool. She looked at both of them. "What can I do to help?"

242

Jaca held the door with his foot. He looked at Peterson. "Are you coming?"

Without a word, Peterson entered the elevator with Jaca and Gloria Sheaffer.

After lengthy and emotional phone calls to New York and the Company officials, it was done very quickly. Captain Coldwater was ordered that under no circumstances was he to shoot anyone. He was ordered to give in to the demands of the students. With Jaca and Colonel Peterson acting as counsels, Peterson for the students and Jaca for Coldwater, agreement on just one point was achieved: no charges of any kind would be brought against any persons under any conditions. Coldwater, as master of the S.S. *New York* accepted all responsibility, admitting that he might have provoked the students, and that he might have unwittingly, and through ignorance of conditions aboard his command, reacted hastily, and the students were therefore justified in their acts.

As a final act of surrender, Peterson (acting for the students) demanded that Coldwater resign. Coldwater refused. He would, however, allow himself to be put on the sick lists, which was acceptable to all sides. Coldwater wrote the log himself as the great

243

ship approached the New York track to Ambrose light.

> Captain Abraham Coldwater on orders from ship's medical officer, was relieved of his command at fourteen thirty-three hours September 3, 1969. Chief Officer Reggie injured (as noted by the log), command of the vessel has been given to Second Officer J. Trapp.
>
> Abraham Coldwater

It was finally over. There was nothing in writing. The public relations firm handling the Company's account released a version of the incident that made Indian's victory complete:

> Reports of a student mutiny aboard the S.S. *New York* were proven false today with the ship proceeding on schedule to New York.
>
> Captain Coldwater, master of the S.S. *New York* confirmed by ship-to-shore telephone that there had been minor frictions between the ship's crew and the students, but dismissed the reports as being exaggerated. "Nothing more than the high spirits of youth," Captain Coldwater said. "A very smooth crossing."
>
> The S.S. *New York,* the largest passenger liner in the world, holds the transatlantic speed

record. With three swimming pools, nine bars,
ten dining rooms, the vessel represents the
finest ocean travel in the world.

There was a brief triumphant celebration in G-
703. Cora, Indian, Fatso, Ugly, Big Mouth, Film
Maker, Ling Jung, Ralph Rome and the bike security
roared and screamed and yelled and hugged and
kissed and laughed and cried.

Then Indian called for quiet. And like Washington
giving his farewell address to his officers, Indian
spoke to the last meeting of the North Atlantic Students Redress Assembly.

"There are a few details I think we should take
care of before anything else. Take the typewriters
we used for cutting the stencils and throw them
over the side. The mimeograph machine as well, and
all the paper and any evidence that there was an
active," he paused and looked around at them, "conspiracy." He paused again. "That's the only thing
we have to be afraid of now. Dig?"

Everyone nodded.

" 'Kay. The war is over. *For now.*" He smiled his
charming smile. "When you leave here, take a bath,
change your clothes and get lost in the crowd. Don't
speak to each other again. This is it. And I want to
tell you how beautiful you are." Indian then went to

245

each of the group and hugged and kissed each of them. The girls cried. The bike security, too, cried openly. Then one by one they slipped out of the cabin, leaving only Ralph Rome, Cora and Indian. "That goes for you too, *numero uno*," Indian said. The two young men embraced and held each other.

"Let's keep in touch, man," Ralph Rome said.

"Sure, sure — when you see me up on the sky-line."

"Hang tough, man."

"You too, Number One."

"Chief?"

"Yes, Ralph?"

Ralph Rome could not speak. "Groovy, man," he whispered and hurried out of the cabin.

In G-703, Indian turned to Cora. His eyes flashed. He stroked her thigh. He touched her breasts. He kissed her. He had won. It was all behind him. And it meant absolutely nothing to him. "Let's groove," he said.

He had no idea of what was going on aboard the ship after the surrender, and he did not care. Cora sensed his total indifference. But action freaks were her bag and what could she do about it? It was her *thing*.

She undressed quickly, quivering.

246

9

Washington
Would Have Given His Life
to Have These Students
with Him at Valley Forge...

THE HUDSON RIVER PIER which the S.S. *New York* used as its home port was over a thousand feet long; a huge terminal, built during the late depression in the WPA Utility Style, whose exposed girders created a fine lacy green filigree supporting a distant, forbidding black roof. A regular procession of skylights across the roof was of no use at all. Pigeons lived in the lofts; whole flocks wheeled about the emptiness of the upper spaces. Many of them had never flown outside the pier. They fought their cohabitants of the underworld, the wharf rats, for the poverty prizes of garbage and spilled foodstuffs. These pigeons, isolated, had developed in the short period of thirty-five years special characteristics to survive. It was not uncommon for a sailor returning down the lonely pier to see them dive-bombing the rats out of the darkness above, swooping ninety feet like projectiles to steal some morsel of food. Some-times the rats would stand on their hind legs and defend their food, snapping at the pigeon with their teeth. The rats nearly always lost.

As one approached the pier, heading west toward the Hudson on any of several cross-town Manhattan streets in the Fifties, it presented a huge opening, a maw, a cavern, the prehistoric omnivorous primary ingestive aperture. It was frightening — until one spotted the even larger, pennant-bedecked, beauti-fully groomed S.S. *New York*. It would reassure the traveler to see the more presentable art and works of man, so that with no courage at all required, he could, literally, enter the pier.

But the pier presented no test of courage that afternoon. It was the appointed place for wives, mothers, fathers, sisters, brothers, uncles, aunts, friends, business people and others to reclaim their loved ones from the great ship.

From the first moment that the message from the North Atlantic Students Redress Assembly hit the international public awareness, the pier had been besieged by hundreds of people. At first there was an air of desperate anxiety, charged with the tension of those concerned, who asked questions, demanded answers from Company officials, police, pier guards, customs men, immigration officials — anyone who

wore a uniform or had an officious manner. Then
slowly the sheer weight of time began to wear them
down. The earlier desperation wore thin and irrita-
tion came in its place. There were worried parents
from the middle class, who saw the incident as just
one more that their child had become involved in and
that they could not understand and that they would
have to pay for; aggressive, upper-middle-class parents who carried themselves as though they could
wield a degree of influence they did not possess and
never would; assorted aunts, uncles, girlfriends and
boyfriends questioned, demanded, refused to give up.
Collectively, the greeters became a slightly hysterical
boorish mob with fear very close to the surface.

Several distraught fathers decided to take on the
pier security guards and a few mothers backed them
up. They lost. It was a scene of gut reactions. Every
filthy oath and threat, every manner and behavior
Indian had so carefully programmed for his people
aboard the ship, was offered up spontaneously here.
Within an hour of the great ship's arrival at the pier,
they had to call out New York's finest; and a few
mothers and fathers, very much *now* concerned,
were busted. But the rats and the pigeons loved it.
There were a lot of uneaten sandwiches, hot dogs,
cigar butts and half-finished bottles of Coca-Cola
(rats were expert at tipping over the bottles and

lapping up the sugar water). Finally the precinct captain, being annoyed with humanity that night, ordered the pier closed. But that order soon had to be rescinded. The loved ones spilled out into the street, blocked traffic, and worst of all were suddenly accosted by pickpockets, prostitutes, ice-cream vendors and a few muggers; there was one semiserious moment when the police took on a group of Blacks who had come down to protect any of *their* people who might be passengers aboard the great ship. And even that incident was forgotten when one of the anxious mothers was mugged and dragged into a side street and raped in the back of a parked car. At that point the precinct captain decided to let the loved ones back onto the pier. Another problem arose when tiresome TV news reporters and cameramen wanted to be able to go everywhere and see and hear everything; a very high city official was required to come down and negotiate what could be done about that.

The cotton-candy press release on the war aboard the S.S. *New York* put out by the Company's public relations firm had not fooled those who were concerned with such matters. The FBI, the federal agency concerned with investigating crimes committed at sea on American vessels, had swarmed aboard the ship back at the pilot station; Coast Guard officers, directly responsible for the licensing of all American seamen, followed close after them; Company officials, insurance adjustors, interior decorators, shipyard fitters, engineers and surveyors followed each other in a steady file up the sea ladder.

There are no bicycle paths or walkways on the Verrazano Bridge but hundreds of motorists stopped their cars and watched as the great ship moved into the Narrows and on up the harbor, passing the Statue of Liberty and then into the Hudson River. Belowdecks, led by a no-nonsense inspector of the FBI, the investigation, the questions, the digging in, went on. All of the very best FBI techniques were used, including isolation and a super-smooth intimidation of witnesses, in attempts to sniff out a criminal conspiracy, but it came to nothing. The passengers in first class and second class and the students had nothing to say. At first the crew pointed out individual students who had assaulted them in the general melee, but equal accusations were made by students against crew members. All everyone wanted to do was to get the hell off the ship and forget about it. By the time the tugs had taken hold of the huge ship and started the delicate maneuver of getting it into the slip, no one would identify anyone, no one would say what had happened more than that the students had done this or that, but never, after the pressing, however gentle, of the interrogating agents, would they point to any individual student as being responsible. There was nothing to be done. The Coast Guard decided it would hold a major investigation and the FBI contented itself with photographing every passenger as they prepared to leave the ship. By the time Finished-With-Engines was rung on the ship's telegraph, the ship was quiet and the Company had a preliminary estimate of seven and a half million dollars and six weeks for the ship to be refitted and returned to regular transatlantic service.

"But, Colonel Peterson," the FBI agent protested, "as one of the negotiators, acting for the students, you must have talked to someone about what to do — or accept — or reject when the truce was worked out —"

"I talked to a lot of them. A hundred — at least," Peterson said.

"Can you identify them?"

"I don't think so. I'm very tired." Peterson shrugged. He saw absolutely no reason in the world to take this thing any further.

"Colonel Peterson, I think you're being evasive."

"Think what you want. My whole point of view was to stop the fighting and the potential of bloodshed — murder if you will — because that is what it would have been. The students were never armed at any time with more than chair legs or water hoses. The crew and officers of this ship wore *sidearms*. Dr. Jaca and I were concerned with one thing only — *stop the fighting*."

"We're only trying to get to the facts, Colonel," the FBI agent said.

"Look, I'm very tired. My daughter is dead. I've been through a great deal. If you really want to pursue this thing further, you have my address and the name of my next superior officer —"

"We'll certainly be in touch, Colonel," the FBI agent said crisply. "Thank you."

Colonel Algernon Peterson pulled the zipper on his bag and looked one last time around his cabin. Elienne's things had already been removed to the companionway by the cabin steward (who had a huge welt over one eye). The acrid odor of scorch from the fires pervaded the whole ship; in second class, where the air conditioning had stopped working thirty-six hours before, it was very strong. He lit a cigarette, tasted it and then put it out. Colonel Peterson could not move. He sat down on the side of the bed and tried, very hard, to make sense out of what had happened to him in the past four days. He had come aboard the ship with his daughter with all the expectations that a man could have in his position.

"Stop it," he said to himself aloud. "If there is any-

255

thing to be done now, without regrets, then do it for Elienne — listen to them — really *listen*."

He stood. He picked up his bag. "For you, dear, for you, from Papa, I'll listen to them —" From outside he heard a tug whistle. It was not unlike a distant train whistle, begging you to come away and see the world.

He opened the door and merged in the crowd leaving the ship, and went below to the hospital to sign the necessary papers for the release of his daughter.

Ralph Rome, clean-shaven, in a clean shirt and jiggling coins in his pocket, stood on deck watching the activity on the pier and talked with the FBI agent. "Man, I want to tell you it was a wipe-out. You never *saw* anything like it in your whole life. They were beating up on our people — look, look at this!" Rome displayed a bandaged arm and a cut on the back of his neck. "That's what it was like, man. The crew went apeshit, you know what I mean? *Ape!* What are you going to do when somebody starts beating up on you? Huh, I ask you. Shit, man, you let some sea jock hit you and you hit back, man. *Hit back!* Anytime!"

"When was the first time that you observed any hostility on the part of the crew —"

"The morning they served us rotten eggs," Ralph Rome said. "They laid some heavy sea-jock muscle on us and we wouldn't take it. I mean, like we paid our fare, right? They didn't get rotten eggs in first class. They just dumped on us, down in tourist, so —"

"Did you ever talk to anyone about doing anything — together — in retaliation?"

"Are you crazy? We were at sea, man! It's mutiny, ain't it? I mean to go up against the rule of the sea!"

"May I have your full name and address, please?"

Sir Harry and Lady Weldon stood ready to leave amid the disorder of the Arcadia Suite. "I've never wanted to get away from anything so desperately in my life," Sir Harry said.

"Dear —"

"Yes?"

"Do you have the Argentina bag?"

"It's with the others," Sir Harry said. "Are you ready?"

"Dear —"

"Yes?"

"Dear, why did they do it?"

"Does it matter, darling? Does it really matter?"

"I would like to think that it does. But then —"

"Of course, but then —" Sir Harry said. "Come."

With shrill cries the loved ones pointed and signaled and punctuated their recognition with violent
waves of the arm, crowded down on the pierside as
they spotted their kith or kin. The immigration people had their hands full with the foreign students,
and the customs people were watching out for pot
and hashish and speed, and the Company officials
were trying desperately to spot those in first and
second class who might have damaged luggage or a
bruise or a bandage, then hurrying them as gently as
possible to a special trailer set up on the pier where
insurance adjustors were ready to pay spot cash for a
signature of waiver. They were doing big business.
The FBI, silent, anonymous, was taking photographs; and Coast Guard officers, genuinely aware of
the near-miss of a tragedy at sea, were listening for
anything that might help them shape new regulations.

Fat Cat, Ugly, Big Mouth and Film Maker waited in
a crowd of other students on the main deck as their
papers were checked. The FBI observed them, occa-
sionally picking almost at random an individual student and taking him or her aside for a quick questioning.

"You know," Ugly said, "I don't think I'll ever
forget any of you as long as I live."

"Say that again," Fat Cat replied. "But I've got different ideas —"

"Like what?" Big Mouth asked.

"Never mind."

"No, tell us," Ugly said.

"Well, you're going back to Ohio, right?"

"Yes."

"Cleveland?"

"Yes."

"It's on my way to Duluth," Fat Cat said, making his point.

Ugly nodded. She nodded again. She looked at Big Mouth. Big Mouth got the idea; she eased forward in the line and left them alone.

"I had to dump all my exposed stock," Film Maker said.

"But why!" Big Mouth demanded. "It was so important!"

"Fuck you," Film Maker said easily. "That stuff I shot was in case we couldn't get out of it alive. But we are. He handled it pretty smooth, you know?"

"Smooth my ass," Big Mouth said. "Just because we're not getting busted?"

"That's it," Film Maker said. "He's a golden man. One of a hundred that's going to come along, one way or another —"

"Shit," Big Mouth said. She advanced to the card

table that had been set up and produced her passport and health card. She smiled at the handsome FBI agent standing to one side.

"Did you expose any film on the trip?" the FBI man asked Film Maker hopefully, ignoring Big Mouth.

"No stock," Film Maker said. "Can you beat that? Me with a Bolex and a lens I picked up in Switzerland that oughta cost at least three hundred — and I haven't got any stock to shoot the only thing that ever really happened to me in my whole life."

"What do you mean?" the FBI agent asked, casually offering Film Maker a cigarette while his pale blue eyes swept the crowd.

"I mean, when is a film maker going to get a chance to shoot the kind of action we had aboard this boat? Right? It couldn't happen again in a hundred years?"

"Why not?" the agent asked, lighting his own cigarette. "Why couldn't it happen again?"

"Because, man, don't you see! It's all behind us."

"Passport, please."

"Just a moment," the agent asked. "Why couldn't it happen again?"

"Because you're going to change the laws, right, man?" Film Maker said.

260

But Lulu Tennington's husband had photographs. They were still pictures, but they were sensational. *Life* and *Look* editors were aboard dealing with anyone and everyone that might have photographs; and when they found out that a professional cameraman had over a hundred rolls of tri-X high-speed exposed film using a Yamacraw with a two-seven lens, they started to deal even before Lulu Tennington's husband was finished packing. And with all this interest centered on her husband, Lulu Tennington, Texas, oil, decided not to divorce him after all, and forgot all about Joe Trapp, Second Officer.

Jaca stood at his desk. He had answered so many questions that he could not think anymore. He watched as the smooth-cheeked and smooth-talking FBI agent read and reread the mimeographed sheet of the North Atlantic Students Redress Assembly — Demands.

"It is very cautious," the agent said.

"What is?"

"The whole address." The agent held up the sheet. He read it again. "This last paragraph. It's a disclaimer."

Jaca said nothing.

"And you have no idea who put this out — or why?"

"I have an opinion on both points," Jaca said.

"Would you tell me about it?"

"You wouldn't be interested. It deals with philosophy, Mr. Agadjion."

"I would like to hear it."

"There is a current in the world, an electric current, if you will; it means that the world is —" Jaca stopped. He looked up at Gloria who stood in the doorway, beautiful, beautifully dressed. She carried a small dog in her arms. Jaca walked to her side. He held out his hand to the dog, which licked his fingers. "What do you call it?"

"It's a young lady named Putzi," Gloria Sheaffer said.

"Where will you be?"

"Plaza," she replied.

"Miss Sheaffer, isn't it?" the agent said, intruding.

"Yes."

"Can you tell me anything about the trip?"

"Yes. A great deal," Gloria Sheaffer said. "I had a sick headache and cramps."

"I mean —"

"I was constipated and vomited most of the time. Have you ever experienced that?"

The agent backed away, slipping back into the professional attitude of no argument.

262

She tucked Putzi under her arm and walked away. Jaca turned back to the FBI agent. "Is there anything else?"

"Dr. Jaca, since you're named in this Demand — what have you got to say about it?"

"Foolishness," Jaca said tiredly.

"How do you mean?"

"My God, man!" Jaca said. "I'm vulnerable. I'm a doctor. I had a patient die on the trip. She happened to be a young person, she had taken LSD and her heart couldn't take the strain — they decided I would be a good target. Doctors are, you know."

"You're a Cuban?"

"American."

"Did you ever know Fidel Castro?"

"Once."

"Have you been in contact with him lately?"

"No," Jaca said. "Nor was I in contact with Che, nor have I been —"

"Dr. Jaca," the agent said quietly, "we only want information. We're not out to persecute anyone."

"Information. Yes. Of course. Fishing for information."

"You mentioned a philosophical answer to my earlier question."

"What was the question?"

"Who put this Demand out," the agent held up the paper, "and why?"

"Oh, yes."

"Philosophical, I think you said, Doctor."

"Do you want it all at once or a little at a time?" Jaca asked.

"Any way you want to tell it, Doctor," the agent said easily.

"Take this down," Jaca said, waving his hand airily.

"I'll remember it," the agent said.

"We're in a world crisis. It has been going on since about the middle of yesterday."

The agent looked at him quickly. "Yesterday?"

"Shocked you, didn't I?" Jaca said with a smile. "Philosophy, Mr. Agadjion, deals with the study, or science if you will, of the truths and principles underlying all knowledge and reality. They, the students, are a reality."

"Yes?"

"You're dealing with them as though they were criminals!"

"That is an assumption, Dr. Jaca. We're only an investigative agency and as such we draw no opinions."

"That's possible," Jaca said.

"Probable."

"All right, probable — so what?" Jaca responded tiredly. "Look — I will not either condemn or condone what happened aboard this ship during the past

264

four days. It happened. It exists. It existed. The two points, in case you've forgotten them, are as follows. They had something to say. They chose this way of expressing themselves. You or I or society may not agree, but you must admit, if they had drunk their milk and been nice kids the past trip, you wouldn't be here now. Now you know about them —"

"Did they threaten you, did any individual ever threaten you?" the agent asked.

"I have been threatened many times."

"But this trip, now, in these circumstances, Dr. Jaca. After all, you've got to admit that your name is specifically mentioned in their redress demands. Did anyone threaten you?"

"No."

"Not at all?"

"No."

"Not even philosophically?" The agent smiled.

"I am challenged every day of my life with the need to find a new and better way to the truths of life."

"Thank you, Dr. Jaca." The agent stood. "You'll be hearing from us."

"Don't call me, I'll call you," Jaca said.

"Good-bye, sir."

"Good-bye," Jaca said. He turned to the hospital where Nurse Claudet was helping Kenneth, Nurse Carol and the ambulance doctors with Mrs.

265

George Bedford. Jaca walked to the side of the old lady and took her wrist. No change. The pulse barely whispered up to him as it had done when she came aboard, but her eyes were clear.

"You never did come back for my life story," she said. "I used to think it was dirty, until I met some of the young people who were brought in here. My God, I'd have given all my millions to have been up there with them —"

"Good-bye."

"I'd ask you to come see me —" Mrs. George Bedford said as they rolled her out, "but I know I won't live until you come. But remember this — nothing has changed. Nothing."

"Yes, I will remember," Jaca said. He leaned over and kissed the parchment cheek.

There was one really fine moment amid the chaos. A young vice-president in the Company who was much more attuned to the action than anyone else, took it upon himself to rent a house trailer which he had towed onto the pier, and with Toots Shor catering, he set up a bar and invited everyone. It was a very thorough and thoughtful thing to do; he even went so far as to have a sign painted, which was draped over the entrance:

DON'T DROP OUT, DROP IN

The bike group received a lot of attention from the investigators, but like all the other students, they knew nothing except that they reacted as anyone else would have done when the crew started in on them. It soon became apparent to the investigators that the initial incident started in the tourist dining room on the second day and that it had escalated from there, with overreactions on both sides, building to the final outrage in the first-class swimming pool, which triggered total war. No one knew anything about the mimeograph machine, or where it was, or what typewriters were used. The bike security stood around on the pier regaining their sense of aloofness from the other students and waited for their bikes to be unloaded. Then, adjusting their gas feeds, with a stuttering and popping of exhausts they rode off the pier and disappeared.

Aside from Indian, who received the most attention of all, Ling Jung was questioned longest: the investigators spent more than an hour with him as he packed his bags.

"Why were you selected to talk to the captain?" the agent asked.

"Because I speak Chinese," Ling Jung said.

"Does the captain speak Chinese?"

"I don't know, man. I didn't ask him."

"You're being evasive," the agent said.

"Don't be smart-assed, man," Ling Jung said. "There were a lot of heads busted on this ship and all I was trying to do was stop it."

"Do you know how it started?"

"Sure. Rotten eggs. Then they started giving us a hard time, and the next thing you know it's a mixer."

"Why did you try to stop it?"

"Seen much blood in your life, man?"

"A little."

"I seen a lot of it, you know? I mean — blood. I don't like violence and violence means blood —" Ling Jung shrugged. He had finished his packing. He sat on his bunk and stared at the agent, being inscrutable. He lit a cigarette.

"Did you see anyone smoking pot?" the agent asked.

"What's pot?"

"Speed?"

"What's speed?"

"Hashish?"

"I don't understand."

"Why did you demand that the one they call Indian be released from confinement?"

"Not only Indian," Ling Jung said, "but all the others as well. Who can say who did what to whom? They just grabbed off a bunch of guys and leaned on 'em — it didn't make any difference to the crew."

"Why not?"

"Well, hell, man, you know, we all look alike, don't we? With the long hair and beads and stuff."

"Did you know Indian before coming aboard the ship?"

"Never saw him before in my life," Ling Jung said.

"Give me your home address please," the agent said tiredly.

Indian sat back on his bunk with his back to the wall and stared at the three agents arranged on the opposite bunk. "I am not a member of the SDS, nor am I a Communist, nor do I belong to any student union, or anything but Phi Beta Kappa. I came aboard this ship anticipating a nice relaxing trip home before continuing my studies. I was in the dining room on that first morning at sea. I was served rotten eggs. I vomited. A girl vomited — a lot of us vomited. The waiters wanted us to clean up our vomit. We refused. Somebody threw something and we threw something back. That's how it started." Indian sighed. He smiled. "Before you knew it, there was a general feeling of antagonism between the crew and the students. It was natural, I think. With a lot of the kids, expecting a good groovy time going home, to suddenly find that a girl had lost a tooth, or a guy had a busted head because some illiterate ape sailor got out of hand and couldn't be controlled by their officers — who I think are really responsible."

"Did you have anything to do with the formation of the North Atlantic Students Redress Assembly?" one of the agents asked.

"No," Indian said. "Like everyone else aboard, I picked up one of the mimeographed flyers and that was it."

"What was it?"

"Action," Indian said. "We'd been given a hard time and some of the kids decided to resist, I guess. I don't know."

"Why were you arrested?"

"Because I was standing there and they just started grabbing bodies."

"What was the difficulty you had with Colonel Peterson?" one of the agents asked.

"No difficulty at all. I opened my door and there she was, freaked out. My roommate, whom I didn't know at the time, and a girl, Cora Ingersoll, were trying to help her. Colonel Peterson came on strong and beat hell out of all of us. Including Miss Ingersoll."

It went on and on. For more than three hours, with Indian telling them everything just as it happened, except his part in it.

Little by little the ship quieted. The passengers had nearly all departed. The FBI agents had left the ship, and the Coast Guard was making a preliminary survey of the emergency lifesaving equipment, and the crew (after signing off articles) was allowed to go ashore. There was only a standby watch aboard. The first of the cleanup crews had not yet arrived. The great ship was scorched and burned and quiet; like a magnificent race horse that had pulled up lame and exhausted, the ship lay aberth at rest and in agony.

Jaca finished his packing. He wasn't going to take everything, just his best suits and shirts and personal things. Nothing that would remind him of the last four days. He wanted to forget it. He didn't want to think about it anymore. He snapped the locks on his bag and turned to the door. Captain Coldwater stood staring at him. "Abe —" Coldwater's face was gaunt, drained.

"I'm glad I caught you, Luis," Coldwater said.

"I wasn't going to leave without seeing you," Jaca said.

"Come'n, I'll walk you to the gangway."

271

They picked their way through the rabble in the companionways, the smell of scorched and burned material stinging their nostrils. "It's easier out on deck," Coldwater said. "You can't get through the second-class lounge." There was a pause.

"What happened?" Jaca asked.

"Nothing, really. I'm retired. I'll get my pension."

"And your papers?" Jaca asked, not wanting to know.

"Temporarily suspended until the investigation." Coldwater shrugged. "But you know how that will end. I'm beached."

"I'm sorry, Abe," Jaca said. "I'm really sorry."

"I could understand it a lot better if there had been something for them to gain. Anything —" They went through the French Room. It had been partially cleaned up: there was a path through the burned rubble. Then they were on deck again, overlooking the pier shed and, farther up, the skyline of Manhattan aglow and beckoning.

"How about you?" Coldwater asked.

"Well, of course I'm finished here — and with the ships," Jaca said. He put his suitcase down. He tried to avoid seeing the scarred and burned ship.

"Why?" Coldwater asked quietly. "*Why?*"

"I don't know, Abe. But somehow I have faith. They're a new breed. He's the coming race. Smart, tough, daring. Washington would have given his life to have these students with him at Valley Forge. It's you and I who are different. They're not different. They're what's now."

"You sound sympathetic — and after what they've done — to the ship — to you — and me."

"I am sympathetic," Jaca said. "Like it or not, they're the future. And you've got to admit, he did a beautiful job. Clean as a whistle."

"If they're the future, then I'm glad I'm old. I'm just sorry, really sorry, that they took away my ship."

Coldwater turned his face away from Jaca. After a moment, Jaca picked up his suitcase and held out his hand. "Good-bye, Abe."

"Good-bye, Luis."

Jaca stepped away from the railing and to the gangway. He walked slowly down to the pier. He did not look back.

It wasn't Indian, he thought, or even those like him — there would always be Indians, clever enough to lead others. It was society, the entire community of nations throughout the world. Were they going to let the young — the youth — into the mainstream of ideas and leadership, or was there to be a general, universal head-on collision? All the energy and thought that had gone into mere destruction could just as easily have been for something constructive,

273

but the difference — the very subtle difference — is that it would have to be their way.

Well, if their way was better, what was wrong with that?

When Jaca reached the street, his way was blocked by the coffin bearing Elienne's body being taken into an ambulance. Colonel Peterson stood to one side.

"Dr. Jaca," Peterson said.

"Colonel Peterson," Jaca replied.

He caught a cab and, waiting for the light to change, he turned and looked back over his shoulder at the great ship. Then the cab turned the corner and for a brief moment he caught sight of Indian and Cora sitting in a small café laughing and talking.

Special Acknowledgment

The author wishes to thank A. L. Hart, Jr., a perceptive and dedicated editor for his many *aides-mémoire* on this and other books.